The Colour of Memory

Also by Christopher Bowden

The Blue Book
The Yellow Room
The Red House
The Green Door
The Purple Shadow
The Amber Maze
Mr Magenta

The Colour of Memory

Christopher Bowden

LANGTON & WOOD

Copyright © Christopher Bowden 2025
First published in 2025 by Langton & Wood
73 Alexandra Drive, London SE19 1AN
http://www.christopherbowden.com

Distributed by Gardners Books, 1 Whittle Drive, Eastbourne,
East Sussex, BN23 6QH
Tel: +44(0)1323 521555 | Fax: +44(0)1323 521666

The right of Christopher Bowden to be identified as the author of
the work has been asserted herein in accordance with the Copyright,
Designs and Patents Act 1988.

All rights reserved. This book is sold subject to the condition that it shall
not, by way of trade or otherwise, be lent, resold, hired out or otherwise
circulated without the publisher's prior consent in any form of binding
or cover other than that in which it is published and without a similar
condition including this condition being imposed on
the subsequent purchaser.

All the characters in this book are fictitious and any resemblance to
actual people, living or dead, is purely imaginary.

British Library Cataloguing in Publication Data
A catalogue record for this book is available from the British Library.

ISBN 978-0-9555067-7-2

Typeset by Amolibros, Milverton, Somerset
www.amolibros.co.uk
This book production has been managed by Amolibros
Printed and bound by T J Books, Padstow, Cornwall, UK

One

She wasn't good in crowds, never had been. But she had not wanted to miss the reunion, the chance to catch up with her art school contemporaries. A lunchtime event to make it easier for those coming a distance to London had morphed from a sit-down meal in an upstairs room to a free-for-all in the bar afterwards as a well-oiled cohort of artists jostled for space with incoming office workers and a handful of tourists. She was one of the last to leave but then she didn't have far to go.

Putting the racket and buzz of the pub behind her, she looked for somewhere to sit, unwind, gather her thoughts, as the day faded and colour slowly drained away. For a brief while, soft blue light, cool and calming. And that was what she needed on this mid-summer evening.

She spotted a bench under nearby plane trees. It was unoccupied, ready and waiting for her. As she slowly relaxed, she felt soothed by the susurration of the leaves, whispering softly above her, as if sharing the secrets of their day and inviting her to do the same.

How varied the fortunes since they had graduated, she reflected. The best part of thirty years. Some people barely changed, others unrecognizable. The badges helped but she struggled to place many of the names, many of the faces. She wondered if they had the same difficulty remembering her. And then that voice,

"Lucy Potter!"

Sitting on the bench, she relived the moment. She had turned and there was Rex Monday weaving through the throng towards her, glass in hand and a broad grin on his face. She had felt a rush of excitement. She had almost given up hope of him coming. And he seemed as pleased to see her as she was him. She had kept a discreet eye on his progress over the years. A successful print-maker and illustrator, she had seen him on the telly and his work in galleries and bookshops. Stylish but unostentatious, casually smart rather than smart casual, he had retained the full head of hair and boyish good looks that had stayed with her.

Lucy had been talking to a timid-looking woman who rarely ventured, she said, 'up to town', living quietly 'in the country', where she painted portraits, on commission, of children, dogs, and houses. The woman made her excuses and drifted away, perhaps because she did not remember Rex. Or because she did.

He had missed the lunch – 'I had to meet someone in the Far East.' By which he meant Clapton, apparently. 'There *is* life beyond Hackney!' But he did not elaborate and, unlike many men she had known over the years, he asked about her rather than talking about himself.

He seemed genuinely interested and knew she'd had exhibitions in Paris and New York. He had even run across Paul Barnard, the man who had championed her work since spotting her paintings on the walls of a Norfolk tea shop and arranged the show in his Cork Street gallery, Bainbridge and Murray.

"Not that it's there now, of course," she said ruefully. "They finally threw in the towel and joined the others moving east. Though not as far as Clapton."

Rex was just as she remembered, how she had thought of him over the years. More restrained perhaps than the art school showman who had first caught her interest, but that was an act, as she had come to know. Now, it seemed, he was confident enough to be himself, no longer felt the need to perform in public. As she re-ran in her mind their conversation in the pub, she coloured at recollection of her tongue-tied responses – she was nearly fifty for God's sake, not a school girl. Had she been like that when they first met all that time ago? She wondered, yet again, why they had drifted apart, failed to keep in touch, and how things might have been. Or still could be.

She opened her bag on the bench and slipped out the card he had given her. A card! It felt touchingly old-fashioned but it was something tangible – and no shortage of contact details on the back. A studio in Clapton included. On the other side, one of his book illustrations in miniature. A woodcut, in black and white, of two doves on the branch of a tree. She had managed to find one of her own cards, now so rarely used, in the bag's inside pocket. As she gave the card to Rex in return, she thought how garish it looked by comparison. It reproduced one of the colourful abstracts on which she had been working – but not recently. She had done no new work in months. The painter's version of writer's block, she told herself; she was beginning to worry.

Lucy came out of the station later that evening and made her way along the familiar south London streets. It had become warm, sultry, with no hint of a breeze; she was almost on autopilot, her mind elsewhere. The sharp click of footsteps behind her brought her to. They were gaining on her fast. She froze, wondering if she could make it to the corner shop before the footsteps caught her. But the man crossed the road and shot past on the other side. A man in a hurry. He was gripping a large bunch of flowers. At least he has somewhere to go, she thought as the panic subsided, someone waiting for him.

She walked on, unrushed, her progress followed by a watchful moon that had slipped discreetly behind a ragged drift of cloud. After a few moments, she turned into Bardolph Road.

She had passed this way many times before and had no mind to linger now, her first thought being home, and the comforting embrace of an armchair in which she would almost certainly fall asleep. How much had she had? But sudden movement in a wide bay window snatched her attention. She found herself watching figures silhouetted against the light of lamps just switched on inside a room. And as she worked along the row of houses, she became aware of the colours and shapes of other lighted windows. Squares and oblongs and semi-circles of yellow and orange and gold, warm and welcoming yet excluding too, glimpses of lives of which she was not part. The outsider looking in.

Standing on the pavement in the half-light, she felt a keen sense of separation yet compelled to watch a series of vignettes: domestic scenes, unrehearsed performances on undersize stage sets, the window frame as proscenium arch and Lucy Potter an audience of one. Or perhaps not so much audience, since there was no sound, as spectator. She began to fill in gaps, developing plots, supplying mental sound effects, conversations, music. *Act one, scene one: the drawing room of a house in south London on a summer's evening between the wars. A man in blazer and flannels is playing the piano, a medley of popular tunes. Enter through French windows a young woman (auburn hair, moss-green dress, amber beads). She is holding a cocktail glass and looking furtive...*

Part of her felt uncomfortable, conscious that her gaze could be considered intrusive, even voyeuristic. One thing to catch a glimpse in passing, another to stand and stare. On the other hand, if people left curtains undrawn, blinds raised and shutters open, they could hardly complain. She felt a certain transgressive thrill, as if she had been granted privileged access to a forbidden world. And then she wondered if people could see, watch, through her own windows, wondered what they would see, how she would appear, what they would think.

The slamming of a car door broke her train of thought. She sped the last few minutes to Dogberry Road, number thirty-six – her house – coming up dark and empty on the left. She was greeted enthusiastically by next door's Persian cat from his position on the front wall. Engraved in tiny letters on the tag dangling from his collar: *My name is Ozymandias, Cat of Cats*.

Once inside, she switched on the front room light and hurried to draw the curtains.

Two

Lucy sat in the garden the following day, feeling listless, her thoughts drifting back to the reunion. She was surprised that her contemporaries admired her work, surprised that they knew it at all. She was not exactly a household name, had never been attracted to pickled cows or unmade beds.

It was the East Anglian paintings, she reflected, that had established her, graced mugs and tea towels in New York, fridge magnets and birthday cards in Paris. 'Church in the rain', 'Winter trees', 'Willows by the creek', 'Reeds in early morning light'... People liked the subdued colours, a predominance of greys and browns and silvery greens. Melancholy and reflective, they said, with a hint of something more cheerful if you looked: a stripe of yellow ochre on the bark of a tree, a sliver of apricot reflected in water, a smudge of rose pink on the distant horizon.

She smiled weakly at the recollection. The paintings had sold well, she admitted, very well; she could have kept them going. Or churning them out, as she had begun to see it. But she was bored, restless, needed a change, a new lease of life. She had altered course and developed the series of abstracts, geometric, bold, and colourful, quite different from the East Anglian works. They had satisfied her for a while and proved popular with buyers and interior designers wanting a certain look. But they were seen by the critics as derivative. Their comments stung but she knew what they meant. It was time to move on again, do something else. She couldn't stand still.

That was the trouble, she thought, as she shifted in her chair and tried to get comfortable. She needed change to keep motivated. It was never long before she felt stuck in a rut, however lucrative that might be. This time, though, it was taking longer to get out of it. Paul Barnard, her long-time gallerist, suggested she take a break to recharge her batteries, go and stay with her parents at their home in Spain. After all, her father had been an artist himself, would surely sympathise and have some practical advice about unblocking the block. Somehow she doubted it. He had not painted in years and, when active, had produced much the same work throughout. Not that she derided it; quite the contrary. His paintings were part of her childhood – had made her want to be an artist in the first place – and she had some of them on the walls in Dogberry Road. But that didn't help her current predicament.

She had mentioned it to one or two people at the reunion.

"Why not do what Edward Hopper used to do when he got stuck or just wasn't in the mood for painting?" This from the man with the ponytail and the faded denim jacket sitting next to her at lunch. Frank Tardy, the name on this badge. She dimly recalled a younger, slimmer version. He leaned in and sounded confidential. "He went to the movies for a week or more, had a binge and got his mojo back. Gave him ideas for the work too."

"I can't think of anything worse," said Lucy. "Sitting in the dark watching films I don't want to see while everyone else rustles and slurps and spills popcorn on the floor. Sorry; I didn't mean to sound ungrateful."

"How about the buildings themselves? Interiors, exteriors, people milling about – or queuing for popcorn. All over London and beyond. Theatres as well as cinemas, if you like."

"It's not what I do," she said forlornly. "Too much of a constraint. There'd be an expectation that I'd get it 'right', that whatever it was would look like what it was supposed to be. That's not how I go about things. I don't want to produce paintings which simply show people what they can see for themselves. That's not my idea of creativity."

"That's a lot of 'nots'."

"I know. But painting, my painting, has to be about how I see the world, how I interpret it. I just need something to get my teeth into."

Reflecting on the conversation as she sat in the garden, she wished she had sounded more positive.

"Look on the bright side," said Frank. "Most of us have to rely on teaching to make ends meet and fit the painting around it as and when we can. Teaching people whose enthusiasm and ambition greatly outstrip their talent in many cases. If they want to be there at all."

She thought again of her father, who had taught for much of his career and seemed to enjoy it. Even she had had her Thursday Ladies, until good fortune in the form of Paul Barnard had enabled her to focus, propelled her forward. And she had never had to worry about having a roof over her head. So perhaps she was making too much of a few months' loss of transmission.

She went back inside to make some coffee, rootling in a cupboard for Jaffa cakes while she waited for the kettle to boil. She had owned the house, she realised, for over twenty years. She was fond of the place, a two-bedroom terrace bought with her grandmother's inheritance and a loan from her parents at a time when property prices in these parts were a good deal lower. Yet she had lived in it for less than half that time, having decamped to a cottage in Norfolk, more than funded by rent from a series of tenants in the house in Dogberry Road. When she came back two years ago she redecorated from bottom to top and restored the rear bedroom to studio space.

She had held her very first exhibition here, she recalled fondly, as she leant on the kitchen counter, nursing her mug between two hands. It was on a couple of weekends before Christmas only a few months after she'd moved in. A series of watercolours sketched on her travels in Turkey and worked up in final form at home. She remembered the frantic rush to get them framed in time, dithering about where to put them, sorting out the spacing with a recalcitrant metal tape measure, fixing the pictures to the walls. And standing back, exhausted, trying to take it all in; she could still see the watercolours hanging there the night before the exhibition opened.

She had worried that no one would like them, that no one would come at all, leaving her with gallons of mulled wine and boxes of uneaten mince pies. But somehow the word had spread and somehow many of the paintings had sold. Hugh Mullion, in those days a near neighbour, turned up early, she recalled, before she was ready and still making last-minute adjustments. His enthusiasm, his extravagant parallels with other artists. De Chirico, for heaven's sake! He bought two pictures – *A Street in Bodrum* and *Sunset over Zonguldak* – and lent them years later for her retrospective in Cork Street. They were the first paintings she had ever sold.

So much for the past, she thought, snapping back, straightening up. She was not dissatisfied with what she had done, with what she had achieved. But she had to move forward, find some way of unblocking the block. Who was she if she couldn't paint, set down how she saw the world? And, as she well knew, keeping busy had helped to fill the void in her personal life. What were the prospects in that department?

"This Rex Monday," said Clare, through a mouthful

of crab as she reached for a glass of the house white. They were meeting a day or two later in the usual place: Benchers, the wine bar round the corner from her chambers at Number One Partridge Court. Clare Mallory, a barrister once considered 'a promising junior' – rather more years ago than she cared to remember – was Paul's partner and that was how Lucy had met her. Clare's brisk efficiency and keen practical sense never obscured her kind and caring nature, and the warmth of their friendship had sustained Lucy through many difficult times.

"You've not mentioned him before. And you've known him for nearly thirty years."

"We were at art school together," said Lucy, "and met by chance at the reunion."

"By chance?"

"I didn't know he would be there. Not for certain."

"Have you arranged to meet again?"

"No, not really." She sounded forlorn, disappointed, as she was, that he had not been in touch. She kept wondering if she had been wrong, built up her hopes. Not that she had been in touch with him either.

"Not really? Yet you mentioned him before we'd even looked at the menus. Do I detect a degree of discombobulation?"

Lucy felt she was being cross-examined but knew she had brought it on herself. It had all come out in a rush before she had got her thoughts straight.

"Miss Potter. Would you be good enough to tell the court, in your own words, what exactly is going on –

or not, as the case may be." The smile on Clare's face was broadening. She laid a hand, briefly, on Lucy's arm. "Perhaps you could begin at the beginning."

"He breezed in that first day. Everyone stopped what they were doing to look at him. 'My name's Monday,' he said, 'but I'm free any day of the week!' The girls all giggled and the boys smirked."

"He made an impression. Including on you, I take it."

"He was not short of admirers."

"Don't tell me. He attracted women like iron filings to a magnet. Isn't that the expression? So did you and he…?"

"Maybe. Once or twice. A few times."

"Coy *and* discombobulated. A fatal combination."

"Like I said, there was no shortage. Eventually, of course, we all went our separate ways."

"Gone but not forgotten. And then you bumped into him again."

"He'd hardly changed."

"And?"

"He gave me a card with two doves on it. Oh, and he said he'd met Paul."

Clare let Lucy make progress with the crab she had hardly touched and said that Paul was planning a party to mark the first anniversary of the gallery's move to Hoxton. They were just putting together the guest list.

Three

*I*t was early and Lucy was wide awake. An insistent sun was peeking around the edges of the blinds, casting lines of pale yellow on the rug. Another fine day in prospect but what to do with it?

She fumbled for the radio. Abattoirs, genetic modification, giant hogweed, the price of wheat. Important subjects all, no doubt, but not what she needed now. It was not yet six o'clock. She clambered out of bed, lifted her dressing gown from the back of the door, and padded into the studio at the rear of the house.

The corrugated paper taped to the floor, smooth side up, gave it a spongy feel, still disconcerting to bare feet. She eyed the jam jars holding her brushes, some bolt upright, others leaning lazily away from the perpendicular, all unused for too long. Tubes and sticks of oil and acrylic paints lay restless in ice cream tubs. Knives, scissors, and other sharp implements gleamed dully in cane baskets. Her easel skulked in one corner, biding its time. She felt she was being accused, reproached for her inactivity. Her palette, she could not see at all.

She made her way to the large table set at right angles to the window. It was empty but for a pile of sketch books, a loose collection of pencils, and a desk lamp. She sat here every morning for an hour or so, drawing what she saw: a group of jugs, a vase of flowers from the garden, pebbles and other found objects… . Just to keep her hand in, nothing more. But it was still too early. She looked through the uncurtained window, across the garden to the trees beyond, their tops glowing in the strengthening light. They almost seemed to be calling her.

As she was leaving the room she paused by the mantelpiece and picked up the card that was propped against a small pot. She gazed for a few moments at the image on the front, crisp and clear: two doves on the branch of a tree. She did not dwell on the back; she knew the details by heart.

To use the time and help to get her brain in gear, Lucy decided to go for a walk in the woods nearby. The entrance lay at the end of a track that ran from the road in a break between two terraces. Much pitted and puddled on her last visit, the track had since been repaired and now led smoothly to the yew and holly brooding by the gate. Once past, Lucy entered a realm of bird song and green-gold light. Shuffling through dry leaves and twigs, she followed the path to a clearing and sat on a fallen beech trunk. It was pleasingly smooth to the touch.

And as she sat, she felt herself slowing down, felt calmer, detached from her surroundings. Intruding sounds receded: the rustle of a blackbird in the undergrowth, the flap of pigeons far above, the chattering of squirrels chasing along the branch of an ash tree, the low grumble of distant traffic. The stillness became absolute silence, pindrop quiet. She could hear nothing; even her own soft breathing had lost its sound. But the silence was not simply an absence of noise. It was more than nothing. It had an intensity, a weight, a positive quality of its own, though she could not have put it into words. It just was.

What colour was silence? The question had not occurred to her before. A calming, restful one, she supposed. Or was that too obvious? She felt distracted by the variety of greens about her. She dismissed her first thoughts of mother of pearl or a pale duck-egg blue as too wan, too feeble. Silence – this silence – was surely a stronger colour. She was veering towards indigo, toying with matt black, but they seemed too dark, too gloomy. How about ultramarine? Rich and positive but not too intrusive. It struck the right balance. A satisfying thought; she was pleased with that. And then the sudden yelp of an unseen dog shattered the image and the world came back with a jolt.

She shifted on her tree trunk and wondered what she had been thinking about before silence fell and took her away.

It was the woman sitting opposite at the reunion! The one with the Frida Kahlo eyebrows and a butterfly tattoo who said she did things with driftwood and bits of old fishing net. She had suddenly turned to Lucy and asked whether she had a manifesto or mission statement.

"What drives you? What inspires you? What's your vision?"

Her response, she felt, was as unsatisfactory as it had been when Paul had asked for something to include in the catalogue for the Cork Street exhibition years ago. She had come up with an anodyne piece about colour and light and capturing the spirit of place. Anyone could have written it but it didn't matter; the paintings flew off the walls. And that was her point: the pictures spoke for themselves, spoke to the people who bought them. What they saw, what resonated, depended as much on how they viewed the world as on how she did, on their own background and interests and experience. It was a partnership.

"You underestimate yourself," said the woman. "The paintings change the way people look at the world, or slices of it." Had she seen them too? "I'm wondering where you'll go next."

Join the club, thought Lucy, as she got to her feet in the woods and wavered about which path to take. She had wondered, as she lay awake in the early hours, whether the windows she had seen on her way home the other night could be the answer, or at least a stepping stone. Not looking through them to interiors, to private worlds, but focussing on colours and shapes. Not real windows but works of the imagination. And no people.

She didn't do people, not in paintings. They'd get in the way, try to take over.

She found herself carrying on through the clearing, through stripes of alternating light and shade. The path took her gently downhill as hazel coppice gave way to rhododendron on either side, crowding her as she pushed past.

She nearly missed it. Walked ahead, then turned back when she realised she had seen something in the ivy on one side of the path. It was a book, lying face down. One of those old dark-green Virago paperbacks, blending well with its surroundings. *Mrs Palfrey at the Claremont* by Elizabeth Taylor. She had read the book years ago – had been moved by the sadness and gentle humour of it – but not in this edition. She would have remembered the cover, the image of a woman no longer young, sitting with quiet dignity and a hint of melancholy, staring directly at her as she held the book in her hand.

What was it doing here? It was clean and dry, with no hint of morning dew, so could not have lain in the ivy long. But few people would have passed through the woods today and would early dog walkers bring books with them? The book itself was no help: on the flyleaf a name in pencil so faint she could not read it – and a price, 50p.

What to do? Put it back where she had found it and walk on. That was the obvious course. Was it right, though, to leave *Mrs Palfrey* lying on the ground? It seemed disrespectful and left her prey to dogs and foxes and worse. The woman was surely willing her to greater care.

Over the last few months, Lucy had noticed, the area had sprouted a number of 'little libraries'. These took various forms, including miniature glazed cupboards, often fixed to walls. They housed books, which people were free to take, preferably in exchange for ones they left themselves. She found one a short distance from the entrance to the woods. Not a smart new one but a rusting metal cabinet on a pole rising above a garden wall. On the face of it, not a worthy home for *Mrs Palfrey* but it offered shelter and a decent chance for the owner to find her.

The bolt took some jiggling before it slid open with a shudder and a sharp metallic screech. The door was only a little less reluctant. On the shelves, a few detective novels, cheek by jowl with works of historical romance, a couple of almanacs, and a dog-eared *A – Z*. Lying under the bottom shelf, partly hidden by a collection of Middle Eastern recipes, she saw what looked like an old school exercise book. Only fatter. She eased it out to have a better look, wiping away dust and spider's web with a crumpled tissue.

It was a dull object. The plain covers, creased and worn, were reddish-brown or brownish-red. Russet, she thought; a pleasing word and a reassuring colour. They gave the notebook, or whatever it was, an earthy, almost autumnal feel. And it was strangely soft and yielding to the touch with a faintly fungal smell, like mushrooms that were a little past their best. The notebook had clearly been here some time but why was it here at all?

Lucy put *Mrs Palfrey* on a shelf where she had the best chance of being seen and focussed on the notebook. She was reluctant to open it at first, feeling it intrusive, prying into others' affairs, uncertain what she might find. On the other hand, she felt a slight frisson much as she had when catching glimpses of private lives through lighted windows on her way home from the reunion. And the notebook had been left for anyone to find. A quick look would do no harm. Just out of interest. No one would be wanting the notebook back.

She faltered as she glanced at the first page. It made no sense at all. She leafed through the rest of the notebook to see whether the other pages were the same, not that she had intended to read the whole thing. The entire document appeared to be written in what she assumed was some sort of code. Letters and numbers and symbols. Perhaps it was a secret diary! Not unlikely; she remembered Clare once telling her she had kept several teenage diaries in a code of her own devising that had defied her brother's attempts to decrypt them.

Yet this shabby volume did not look like the diary of a teenage girl. And the writing in blue-black ink (did anyone still use fountain pen?) was relentlessly neat and careful with barely a hint of a flourish or any other expression of personality.

She looked for a name and did not find one. But there were some initials (HAW) on the inside rear cover – and an address, both in purple felt tip in a loose and untidy hand quite different from the rest and written much more recently, by the look of it:

53 Brushwood Road

LONDON

SE.

The postcode was incomplete.

She took out her phone and searched for the address. There was only one Brushwood Road in south-east London. She knew where the road was, though she had never been down it. It was not far and she was in no hurry. An intriguing diversion, she thought, a convenient short-term answer to the bigger question of where to go next.

Four

*L*ucy slipped the notebook into her bag and took a shady route to Brushwood Road. It proved to be a street of largish Victorian detached and semi-detached houses with the odd bit of post-war infill.

Forty-five, forty-seven, forty-nine, fifty-one…fifty-five. Fifty-five? She double-checked the number on the front door and went back to do the same with the houses she had passed. There was no number fifty-three. In its place, or where she had expected it to be, the beginnings of a narrow track, flanked by the high walls and fences of properties on either side. The entrance looked well cared for; the grass verges had been mown and were free of litter and other rubbish so that she could walk down it a few yards. But then the cleared area ended and the rest was choked with brambles for as far as she could see. There was no indication of where the track led, or may once have done so.

Lucy felt confused and disappointed, almost cheated, by the absence of the house she had come to find, taunted by the track that took her no further than a thick tangle of vegetation she could not get through. What she would have done if number fifty-three had been in what seemed its rightful place, she did not know. She was only intending to have a look, to see whatever there was to see.

Could she have got the address wrong? She pulled the notebook from her bag to confirm the details and then went back to the street. She looked around for someone, anyone, she might ask about the house. But Brushwood Road was deserted and she was not going to start knocking on people's doors. It was too early in the day to disturb the neighbours, to pester them about a house that wasn't there.

Lucy sat at the table in her studio, staring through the window at distant trees still gilded by the morning sun that was making its way round to the rear of the house. Soon it would hit the acer she had planted ten years ago as a small sapling and which in autumn glowed a spectacular fiery red, at least for a week or two. She had that to look forward to. The sudden appearance of Ozymandias on the fence distracted her. She followed his progress as he jumped down on her side and sauntered, with his usual proprietary air, towards the patch of catnip on which he was accustomed to flop and remain undisturbed.

She turned back to the notebook that was now lying on the table. She had given the covers a gentle wipe with a duster to remove the grime her tissue had missed. They were no more colourful but they exuded a hint of warmth, had a certain rustic charm. Comforting, in a way, she thought, reassuring. The notebook did not draw attention to itself, which could be why it had apparently been left in peace inside the metal cabinet. Russet, she said out loud. She liked that. It felt pleasingly onomatopoeic, like the rustle of leaves in a breeze. Appropriate, perhaps, that she had found it close to the edge of the woods.

None of which explained the mystery of the missing house at number fifty-three. When she got back, she had looked at various maps of the area on-line but nothing showed the gap or the footpath in any detail or at all, other than as empty space. From a satellite view, the whole site appeared overgrown, with mature trees rising at the rear. There might have been something else, something dark among the greenery. She zoomed in and out but the image was too fuzzy and indistinct to be sure.

Odd, she thought, that vacant land should remain undeveloped, particularly round here where demand for property was so high and new housing was crammed in the most unlikely of places. She would ask her friend Hugh if he knew anything about the place and its history. He had lived in the area for years and would jump at the chance to delve into the past.

Today's drawing practice was later than usual. She assembled a group of bottles, pots and jugs, vaguely reminiscent of a still life by Morandi. Not bad, her verdict, viewing the results in her sketch book. Not bad at all – as an exercise. But hardly breaking new ground. She needed to think further about her 'windows' idea, experiment on paper. The finished pictures would need to be a decent size to be convincing, to give at least the impression of real windows. And strong colours, no wishy-washy watercolour. Gouache or oil or what? And how about collage?

She sat back in a quandary. Perhaps a cold drink in the garden would help. Yet what came to her in her seat in the early afternoon sun was unrelated to fenestration or missing houses or russet-coloured notebooks. It was the image of Mrs Palfrey, as Lucy thought of her, sitting quietly by herself in a Lloyd Loom chair in what looked like a conservatory, a gloomy interior beyond. Of course, she was not by herself; she was surely staring at the artist who was painting her portrait a few feet from her. But Lucy could not push away the feeling that the woman was staring directly at her, gently chiding her, less for leaving *Mrs P* alone on a shelf in a musty cabinet than for the current drift or lack of focus in her own life, personal and professional, willing her to do something more positive about it.

A rare thud on the mat as she passed through the hall. She stopped to pick up a small wadge and rapidly discarded the offers from local estate agents to value her property, menus from Indian and Chinese restaurants a surprising distance away, a catalogue of Christmas cards, calendars, and wrapping paper. Already! That left an off-white envelope, too smart to be ripped open between finger and thumb. She took it to the kitchen, opened it neatly with a knife from the drawer, and extracted a thick rectangle of card with embossed gilt lettering.

> *The Directors of Bainbridge and Murray request the pleasure of your company at a reception to celebrate the gallery's first year in Hoxton.*

A date and other details followed.

She felt a mixture of apprehension and excitement, even though Clare had mentioned that an anniversary party was in prospect. She dreaded another round of questions about what she was doing now, her plans for the future, but it would be good to catch up with a different crowd, maybe meet some new people. Mind you, there was only one person she really wanted to see and Hoxton wasn't that far from Clapton, was it? Clare said Rex had been invited but would he turn up?

Five

*L*ucy picked her way down the cobbled side street this warm summer's evening and turned into Hogsden Road. She took care to avoid the yams huddling in the gutter, renegades from the market held earlier that day. She crossed over to the gallery, a nondescript building of pinkish brick and grubby metal window frames. Some called it 'honest', a nod to the area's light-industrial past and a declaration of faith in its future; others called it 'scruffy' and not a patch on the Cork Street premises. Lucy was in the latter camp but she kept her thoughts to herself.

The drone of conversation, peals of laughter, people spilling out to the pavement. She eased through the crowd and entered the gallery. It was a dazzling white box, exposing the original columns, which now supported a mezzanine floor. Barely through the door, she was greeted by Paul's new gallery assistants Hebe and Veronica (use of the term 'gallerina' was discouraged). They were successors to Dido and Belinda whom Lucy had known from the Cork Street days. Both were holding silver salvers that flashed intermittently in the gallery spotlights. One offered champagne, the other a selection of canapés. Balancing bag, glass and something involving asparagus, Lucy penetrated the interior.

She took a sip of champagne and looked round to see if Rex was there. She could not see him among the knots and clusters of guests or make out his voice above the hubbub. Clare had told her he'd accepted the invitation but surely he could not have been and gone already? She rested her glass beside a large vase of peonies in bud, polished off the canapé, and consulted her watch. It was still early, there was still time.

She was briefly distracted by the man in lime-green suit and orange trainers (identified later as street artist Terry Truant), and then spotted Hugh Mullion talking to the elegant Marion Ducasse. She went over to join them. Marion, host of Lucy's successful Paris exhibition at her gallery in the Place des Vosges, greeted her with that familiar brand of restrained warmth – not quite effusive but teetering on the brink. Marion had been listening to what Hugh was saying about Lionel Pybus. How well Lucy remembered the Cork Street retrospective of the work of this forgotten artist, rediscovered some years ago through the joint efforts of Hugh and Lucy herself and dubbed 'the Tooting Kandinsky' by one south London newspaper. A copy of the catalogue they had produced lay on a table nearby.

As if on cue, Paul Barnard appeared among them, looking tanned and relaxed as ever in his trademark linen suit. A man with an air of quiet efficiency and natural authority who did not need to try too hard. After a few words of welcome, he dragged Marion away to meet Terry Truant, leaving Hugh and Lucy to themselves.

While Hebe (or was it Veronica?) topped up their glasses, Hugh was becoming animated. He seemed scarcely able to contain his excitement, bursting to tell her what he had found about the missing house, number fifty-three Brushwood Road. It made her think of a child rushing into his parents' bedroom with a stocking on Christmas morning eager to show what Father Christmas had brought him. Difficult, sometimes, to remember that he was a year or two older than her, had two daughters at university, and held down a responsible job.

And when she mentioned – as she thought, in passing – that the notebook in which she had found the address was written in code, he immediately asked if he could have a go at cracking it, almost put his hand up. She readily agreed with an indulgent smile and steered him back to number fifty-three.

"Those houses," he said with a small air of triumph, "were built in the 1890s on land that belonged to Brushwood Hall. It was demolished to make way for them, sadly. However, the lodge remained, gradually hemmed in by the surrounding development. At some point, the owners of number fifty-one seem to have bought part of the lodge's garden to extend their property. It may be that the remaining site was considered too small to redevelop, certainly on the scale of its neighbours.

"So it looks as though number fifty-three was never built. But the number itself seems to have been allocated, formally or informally, to the lodge at the end of that track you saw."

"Is the lodge still there?" asked Lucy. "Not that anyone could live in it now; the place is inaccessible."

Hugh put his glass down on the table and pulled a piece of paper from his wallet with a flourish. He unfolded it and said,

"I went through the electoral registers. The last entry I could find for this house was in the late 1990s, when the place was apparently occupied by one Gordon Hartley and no one else. Nothing after that for whatever reason. I then had a word with a man I know in the Land Registry. He confirmed that the property remains in the ownership of the Hartley family, specifically Mrs Rosemary Hartley. There's an address for her in Sussex."

Hugh was interrupted by the arrival of his wife, Kate, who had Clare Mallory in tow.

"I hope Hugh isn't boring you," said Kate. "You know what he's like when he gets the bit between his teeth. I'm going to take him away while Clare tells you her news." With that, Hugh pocketed the piece of paper and retrieved his glass, lingering just long enough for Lucy to thank him for all his work and say she would be in touch about the code.

Clare, normally so calm and level-headed, was flushed and breathless.

"He's here!" she said. "I overheard him talking to Paul. They've gone up to the mezzanine."

"Who's here?"

"Rex Monday, of course. He looks just like the picture on his website! Go and talk to him."

"I can't just wander up," said Lucy, courage deserting her as her excitement mounted. "What would I say?"

"Leave it to me," said Clare, taking Lucy's elbow.

Lucy looked at the floor and did not move.

"What's putting you off? His looks or his charm? Come on. Don't let him down; he's expecting you."

"You've spoken to him?"

"Well, somebody had to. I rang him last night to make sure he was coming. I'd say you were pushing at an open door."

Lucy walked slowly up to the mezzanine. She felt nervous, hovering at the top of the stairs before taking tentative steps forward. She found herself gripping the stem of her glass so tightly that she was worried it might break. Rex was talking to Paul, who turned and excused himself tactfully to leave them alone together.

She was struck immediately by the warmth of Rex's smile, the twinkle in his eye. Once again, he seemed genuinely pleased to see her, admired her sparkly blue dress. He admitted that he had looked for her at the reunion, hoped that she would be there, that he would not miss her by arriving late. He said nothing, she noticed, about not having been in touch in the meantime but that no longer seemed to matter; he was here now.

As they spoke about other things, she felt herself relax and sensed that he did too. She began to lose all track of time. She enjoyed his gentle teasing, his quiet humour, the way he held her gaze. He had mellowed over the years; perhaps she had too. But that raffish charm was undiminished. Other women too had fallen for it over the years, she knew. But, after some skirting round the subject, they established that neither of them had anyone else 'just at the moment'. Was Clare right that she was pushing at an open door?

Lucy's memory of the rest of the evening was hazy. She and Rex went to Zog, an Albanian restaurant he knew in Dalston. Yoghurt and cucumber came into the equation somewhere. Of that, she was sure. Stuffed peppers were also implicated and grilled fish almost certainly made an appearance. What they talked about she couldn't remember at all. Perhaps the bottle of Albanian white on top of the gallery's champagne had been a little unwise but she perked up as they walked to the Hi-Hat jazz club a few streets away. She probably imagined that the restaurant's double-headed eagle gave her a wink as they were preparing to leave.

And afterwards?

As she explained to Clare a day or so later, she had never been to Clapton before, just wasn't a part of London she knew. They agreed that it was important to take advantage of the balmy summer months to expand one's knowledge of the capital's highways and byways, even if it did involve an overnight stay.

"So, how was it?" said Clare. "How was he?"

As if the years had rolled away, she said, but calmer and more measured, somehow. She liked being with him, felt comfortable, wanted to be with him. She trusted him – and her judgement about him. But more than that. This did not feel like a casual flirtation on either side and she was excited by the possibilities.

"It could just work."

"I'm really pleased," said Clare. "If you're sure." She hesitated. "You've been hurt before," she added gently.

"I know. But we're a lot closer after our night together. It feels right."

"Two doves on the branch of a tree!" said Clare. "Make sure he doesn't fly off."

Lucy was sitting at the table in her studio the following week, staring sightlessly at the wall ahead. Her sketchbook lay open in front of her, the pages untouched, pencils brigaded neatly to one side. A full mug of cold coffee sat patiently close by.

She looked at her watch. He'd be somewhere over the Atlantic now, had rung from the airport shortly before he boarded. New York, then Boston. Meeting publishers and booksellers, a couple of exhibitions, all arranged ages ago, he said. And he'd be back in a week or two so it was absurd, she told herself, to feel bereft. It had been a while since there had been anyone else; people, she'd thought, had stopped noticing her at all.

She turned to the drawings pinned to the cork board near the door. Preliminary drawings for paintings of windows of various colours and shapes. Had *she* done those? She felt neutral at best about them. But Paul had been encouraging when she mentioned the idea to him, sent him photographs of early efforts. He wanted her to develop a series when she was ready but perhaps not confined to bold and vibrant colours and not all so large as to limit the potential market. Why not work up some further examples and take it from there?

She'd think about it later. Her eye caught the russet cover of the notebook lying on the cabinet next to the table. It remained a puzzle. If number fifty-three Brushwood Road did not exist, or had not been occupied for many years, who had left the notebook in the box near the woods, with the address written fairly recently, by the look of it? She must ask Hugh for the other address, the one he had found for Rosemary Hartley somewhere in Sussex, though what she would do with it was another matter. The name did not even tally with the initials felt-tipped on the inside back cover.

She felt light-headed, her mind a blur as she was pulled in different directions: Rex, her painting, the missing house, the notebook itself. She needed to get a grip, she told herself, sort out her priorities, focus on what was important. She was too passive at the moment, indecisive, prone to distraction. What had happened to the old Lucy Potter, the energetic and successful artist who always liked to be in control?

But she continued to be preoccupied by the code in which the notebook was written, by the possibility or probability that it contained secrets that were not for others' eyes. Otherwise, why write it in code? She had flicked through the notebook several times but was bemused by page after page of apparently random letters, alternating with numbers and symbols. They meant nothing to her.

When she got back from Clapton that first time, the day after the reception at the gallery, she had scanned the first few pages and sent them to Hugh. Despite his willingness and enthusiasm, he'd had no luck, he confessed, in attempting to crack the code, could not detect a pattern or find a way in at all. Then Clare, to whom she'd mentioned it at their last lunch, sent her a message. A barrister in her chambers, she said, was interested in codes and ciphers and how to break them, had written a book on the subject. He was happy to look at the opening pages, to see what could be made of them. When he had a moment.

Six

A few days later, Lucy was in the tea room at the Jacobean manor house of Pyefield Court. She was sitting at a table that wobbled disconcertingly on the herringbone floor as she chased the remains of her carrot cake around the plate. The tea room occupied part of the old stable block and reminders of the building's former use adorned the walls. Saddle racks, hay feeders, horse shoes, sepia photographs of grooms and coachmen from before the First World War. She wondered how many of them survived it.

It had been Hugh's idea to come. He had a meeting that morning, he'd said, with the managers of this and other properties in the south east in his new capacity as a historic buildings consultant. He was still getting used to it after many years working for the Heritage Commission. Pyefield Court was only a couple of miles from the Sussex village of Downing and the cottage occupied by Rosemary Hartley, identified as the owner of number fifty-three Brushwood Road, or what remained of it. Why didn't they pay her a visit, he'd said, see what they could find out?

Lucy wasn't sure what excuse they could make for calling unannounced on someone they had never met. But Hugh seemed unfazed and she was happy to go along with it, have a day out of London, free from the confines of her studio. She knew she should be trying to make progress with her windows paintings but a short break, she told herself, a change of scene, would help her to get back to it with a fresh mind and a fresh eye.

She had enjoyed exploring the grounds: stately oak and ash and the ghostly bark of silver birch, marsh marigolds and drifts of iris along the edge of the pond, the scent of roses and lavender and sweet peas in the walled garden. It brought back memories of summer outings with her parents years ago: handstands and cartwheels on springy turf, playing catch with an old tennis ball, hunting shade with dripping ice creams. After wandering in the heat, it was shade that Lucy needed now. She made for the tea room where she and Hugh were due to meet.

Where was he? The tea room was filling fast. She gave up a chair to the family crowding round the next-door table. She looked at her watch for the third time since finishing her cake. Barely half past three and still only mid-morning where Rex was, his visit unexpectedly extended (he had said on the phone last night) to take in a visit to Portland, Maine. He warned that he might be incommunicado for a while. How long, she wondered, before she heard his voice again?

★

"I couldn't find the exact location of the house," said Hugh, as they turned out of the elaborate gateway of Pyefield Court on to the Downing road. "It's not shown on the map and it seems to be beyond the reach of Street View. But it's somewhere down Fettle Lane. It can't be far."

He slowed as they entered the village, deserted but for a battered Land Rover parked outside the pub, The White Hart.

"Fettle Lane should be up ahead, off to the left," he said, an assessment shared by the disembodied actorly voice that offered directions from time to time. But there was no sign of a turning, apart from the narrow track Lucy spotted just as they were going past. Could that have been it? Hugh turned round by the church and drove back, pulling in by the village shop. Lucy went to explore, reporting that the track was rough and crumbly, quickly disappeared into the beech woods beyond, and had no name that she could see. Shouldn't they ask at the shop for directions?

The sun-tanned woman in the shop greeted their request with a mixture of surprise and wry amusement. Yes, the track was Fettle Lane, and it had once had a sign to prove it. But nobody much went that way now, apart from a few local riders and some serious-looking walkers. She never saw them coming back. It was just about passable by car at this time of year but were they sure they wanted to risk it? Entirely up to them, of course.

"We're looking for Bawson Cottage. Mrs Hartley," said Lucy.

"Rosemary Hartley! Well, good luck with that."

The woman did not elaborate and turned away with a smirk to resume her unpacking of the boxes by the till.

'Down Fettle Lane' proved to be up it. The car climbed slowly, rocking over bumps and into potholes. The narrow road was pinched by high banks of straggly grass and the beech canopy closed steadily above them like the roof of a tunnel. Lucy felt suffocated, fearful. Why were they doing this? Even Hugh was far from his usual Tiggerish self. He sat silent, tight-lipped, as he gripped the steering wheel. Eventually, though, the road levelled out, became wider and less uneven. The sun filtering more intently through the beech leaves lifted the gloom and Lucy's mood. She began to relax.

After a while, Hugh spotted a chimney through the trees and suggested they pull off the road and continue on foot. They soon left behind the smooth grey trunks of beech trees and the satisfying crunch of the mast that covered the ground between them. A fence, then a wall, then a gate and a drive that led from the road and curled round the house that appeared before them.

"Bawson Cottage!" said Lucy, pointing to the flaking sign that clung to the waist-high wooden gate. They stood in silence for a few moments in the warm afternoon light, taking in the brick and flint, the obligatory roses, pink and white, winding round the front door and partially obscuring the windows on either side. A gable to the left, but not the right, made the house look unbalanced in a way that Lucy found mildly unsettling, compounded by the dormers looking down from the roof. A pair of eyes watching them, perhaps warning Mrs Hartley of their approach.

The cottage was set well back, its overgrown front garden bisected by the path leading from the gate. At intervals, yellowing piles of grass lay among old apple trees just coming into fruit.

"Looks like someone is trying to get a grip," said Hugh. "I can't quite picture Mrs Hartley wielding a machete, though. She must have help."

"She could do with some more. Did you discover her age?"

"Eighty-three or -four. So, sixty-odd when ownership of number fifty-three seems to have passed to her."

"I wonder if she ever went back to look at the place," said Lucy, "knows what state it's in."

They lingered by the gate, each, it seemed, reluctant to make the first move. Suddenly, the harsh metallic call of a pheasant strutting across the drive. They jumped, laughed, and Hugh scraped open the gate.

He reached for the front door's cast-iron knocker, a crude representation of a badger, by the look of it, nose pointing down. "Bawson is an old word for a badger," he said, knocking gently. He waited and tried again, harder and then harder still while Lucy peered through gaps in the roses across the windows.

Of Mrs Hartley, there was neither sight nor sound.

"Perhaps she's deaf," said Hugh. "Or at the bottom

of the garden. Or simply reluctant to answer the door to strangers."

"Who could blame her?" said Lucy. "It's pretty isolated. We haven't seen another house. But we don't know she's here at all. There's no sign of a car."

"It could be round the back but would she still be driving? And remember the state of the road from Downing."

"How could she live in a spot like this without one? I can't see her trekking all the way to the village shop – and back. Or anywhere else, for that matter."

As they were returning to the gate, Lucy thought she heard the sound of music, though whether from within the cottage or beyond it she couldn't tell. Just odd notes; nothing that came together as a tune. She turned back and stopped dead. One of the first-floor windows that had surely been closed like the others when they arrived now appeared to be open. She felt uneasy. She had heard no one, seen no one. Had they been under surveillance since they arrived, their every move monitored?

They decided to carry on down Fettle Lane rather than go back the way they had come. It was much more straightforward, joining the main road to London after a few miles of open country.

"I'm sorry you had a wasted journey," said Hugh. "At least I needed to be at Pyefield Court."

"It was nice to have a day out," said Lucy. "And it wasn't wasted, even if we didn't see Mrs H. It put some flesh on the bones somehow."

"The bones of what?"

"Brought her more to life, seeing where she lives."

"If you're right about the window, she didn't want to see us."

"Perhaps; she didn't know why we were there, of course."

"I suppose we could have left a letter or a note," said Hugh. "She'd have been able to consider it in her own time."

"But under no obligation to reply. All a bit impersonal anyway. I wonder what made the woman in the shop smirk when we asked about her."

Lucy paused as a motorbike overtook them with a deafening roar, not far from the junction with the London road. It was the only other vehicle they had seen or heard in Fettle Lane.

A muffled chirrup as they waited at some lights in south London. Lucy pulled the phone from her bag.

"A message from Clare!" she said. "That man in her chambers has managed to crack the code in the notebook. She thinks I should know what he's found."

Seven

*I*t was still light when Clare arrived at Lucy's house that evening and joined her in the garden. Hugh was there too, having brought Lucy back, and intrigued to know what had been found. He was only mildly miffed that Clare's colleague had cracked the code that had defeated him.

"It's not all of it," said Clare, pulling a buff folder from her briefcase. "Just the first page or so of what we gave him. Toby will look at the rest when he gets back from his hearing in Warwick but he thought you ought to see what he's found so far. The code is not without interest in its own right, he told me, but what really caught his attention is what the thing actually says. 'A trifle disturbing', was how he put it. Toby is given to understatement."

Clare removed a typewritten sheet from the folder resting on her knees. "I think it best," she said, sounding oddly formal, as if speaking at a chambers conference, "if I read this out loud, particularly as there are two of you. I've had a chance to look at it already so I know what to expect. I'll leave this copy with Lucy when I go."

She took a sip of water, cleared her throat, and began to read.

> *It was Father who let me out. He had come home unexpectedly and she had not thought to pocket the key as she usually did, had left it in the door. In truth, it was not uncomfortable in the cupboard under the stairs, cramped as it was. A fraying patch of carpet between the Hoover and the boxes kept, she said, because they might 'come in'. And a pile of rags torn up for cleaning; old towels mostly, a few of Father's discarded shirts. I had learnt to smuggle things under a cardigan, in a pocket – a bar of chocolate, a book, a small torch to read by – squirrelling them quickly behind the boxes when I heard the harsh click of the key returning to the lock. It began to feel more like a nest than a prison cell.*
>
> *She always invited me to choose my punishment – she called it 'making amends' – and this seemed no worse than the others on offer. Whenever I answered back, as she put it, disagreed with what she said or suggested or did, showed some capacity for independent thought. She claimed, of course, that it was for my own good. She was protecting me from myself. Nobody liked an argumentative girl, she said, one with ideas above her station. Trying to be clever. She meant someone with the temerity to have views or ambitions or aspirations.*
>
> *Later, much later, I came to think that she saw me as a threat, feared that any success on the part*

of a daughter would underline her own narrow existence, her failure to achieve whatever ambitions or aspirations she may once have had for herself. Hence her determination to ensure that I did not outshine her or do anything much at all. But at the time I accepted it as normal because I knew no other, had no basis of comparison.

I was an only child and did not meet other children. She said they would be a bad influence. So I was not sent to school, not then. She taught me to read and write and do simple arithmetic. Later, some geography and history and drawing at the kitchen table. It was Father who showed me plants and birds and insects in the garden, put names to them. He asked me to make lists of what I saw, to illustrate them with sketches of my own. I kept them in my room; the ones I gave my parents were not put on display at home. He told me years afterwards that he had saved them all, preserved them in a cabinet in his office.

And he introduced games: croquet on the lawn when the weather permitted, cards or board games indoors. She a reluctant participant and only when Father was there too. A small glint of triumph on her face if I was sent to jail as we played Monopoly. Hours of solitaire for me on a green baize table in a corner of the conservatory. We did not play Happy Families.

No one said anything for a while after Clare stopped

reading and slipped the document back into the folder. It was Hugh who broke the silence.

"Disturbing is putting it mildly. All the more for being so matter of fact. And this is just the beginning. How much more is there?"

"Toby, Clare's colleague, has a bit more but it fills a whole notebook," said Lucy. "I only have the one; maybe there were more originally and this is the sole survivor."

"I wonder when was it written, how old she was when these events took place," said Hugh. "And why she wrote it. It can't be the girl's diary. The language is too sophisticated and feels as if it was written long after the events she describes. Looking back as an adult."

"That struck Toby too," said Clare. "No child could have devised this code, he said. Nor many adults for that matter. And the handwriting itself is clearly the work of a grown-up. Neat, methodical, no sign of a mistake."

"Page after page of letters, numbers, and symbols, in any number of combinations," said Lucy. "But all set out in groups of four. It's strangely meticulous, disciplined, when you consider what she was saying, what she endured. Relentless, somehow. Driven."

"But consistent with the curious matter-of-factness of the piece," said Hugh. "Why do it at all, though? What prompted her to write it years later and why in code?"

"Cathartic, perhaps," said Clare. "Getting it out of her system and written for her eyes only."

"Just for herself?" said Hugh. "It's oddly descriptive in places. I wondered for a moment if it might be a part of a memoir. Or even a novel or a short story. But I can't reconcile that with going to the trouble of devising a code and putting the whole thing in it."

"Let's see what the next instalment brings," said Lucy, as Clare stood up and handed her the sheet. "If we can face it. How much worse can it get? Thank Toby for me, won't you?"

After Clare and Hugh had left, Lucy poured a glass of the chilled white wine which they, as drivers, had declined and went back to the garden. She sat in the fading blue light, hints of pale turquoise and apricot already visible between the trees. She envied them their settled relationships, Clare and Hugh. Clare with Paul, Hugh with Kate. She was lucky to know them, to have their support, particularly at the moment when she felt so useless. Neither had changed much over the years, despite the advent of middle age. Clare calm and efficient, Hugh always ready for a challenge and undaunted by setbacks. And scarcely a grey hair between them! Lucy herself had returned to her natural dark brown, having given up on the succession of streaks – magenta, emerald, orange, purple – that used to be her trademark. What she had once thought of as an expression of individuality now seemed dated and a bit embarrassing. And Rex said he liked her hair the way it was now.

She had taken the sheet Clare had given her out of its folder with a view to reading it at her own pace. But it still lay on the table, looking unnaturally white in the gathering twilight. She didn't want to go through it again now, she decided. It was too troubling. It occurred to her that the conversation with Clare and Hugh had focussed largely on mechanics – when and how the thing was written and why. What about the people involved? She felt deeply affected by the girl's plight. It was surely many years ago but it still seemed so real.

How long did the girl have to endure her mother's abuse, what became of her? And what of the mother – she sounded more like the evil stepmother in fairy stories – and the father who woke up late to what was going on? Why did he not know sooner, act sooner? What exactly did he do about it, what was the outcome? He must at least have been complicit in the girl's home schooling.

Could the unnamed girl, she wondered, have been Rosemary? There was no evidence for it, no proven connection between the contents of the notebook and number fifty-three Brushwood Road. The address was in another hand and the initials – HAW – were not even hers. Perhaps Hugh was right after all to suggest that the whole thing was a work of fiction.

Eight

The market in Hoxton was in full swing as Lucy navigated her way through it slowly, carefully, clutching her portfolio awkwardly to one side. She felt exhilarated by the sights and sounds and movement – the gentle wave of brightly striped awnings, the twirl of dresses on hangers, the boxes and bowls of fruit and vegetables, the wedges and rounds and half-moons of cheese, the cries of traders ('pairnd a punnet yer strawbs'), the sizzle of street food warming in pans that looked like overgrown woks.

By comparison, the Bainbridge and Murray Gallery this mild Wednesday morning in late July was an oasis of peace and tranquillity. In fact, the place appeared to be deserted as she peered through the glazed door waiting to be admitted. Not exactly welcoming to casual visitors, she thought, not for the first time. Maybe that was the point. A buzz, a click, and she pushed her way in. Veronica (or was it Hebe?) appeared from nowhere, greeted her warmly, and took her to Paul's office. They passed a series of grid-like abstract pictures in the process of being hung for the gallery's next exhibition. They reminded Lucy of paintings by Mondrian, albeit in colours that might have given him pause – Schiaparelli pink, grass green, a startling mango... . Hommage or hotchpotch? She gulped and went into the office.

Paul was enthusiastic about the contents of her portfolio. She had emailed images which gave him some idea of what to expect but these things, they agreed, were never a true representation of colour or texture, let alone size. She had followed his advice and prepared a range of sample 'windows' pictures in four different sizes, some in gouache, some in watercolour, some bold and bright, others subtle and more muted. One or two included strips of paper, painted over, which gave the pictures an unexpected sense of depth.

"Collage," said Lucy.

"We call it 'mixed media'," said Paul. "The punters prefer it."

"We've got a gap in the calendar early next year," said Paul, after a short interruption to take a phone call from Berlin. "Last week of January, first week of Feb. Terry Truant has changed his mind so you could take his place. And we could trail some smaller pictures at the Christmas show. They'd be a good size as presents. How does that sound?"

"An awful lot of work," said Lucy in a small voice. "Thank you."

"Leave the portfolio with me for the time being and I'll draw up a schedule of the pictures you might do for us and you can see what you think. It might be an idea to go easy on the biggest ones at this stage: excellent for display, less so for carrying home! But, once the word is out, we could get commissions for offices and so on. And I'll do a timetable, like we've done before, covering framing, catalogue, posters, cards, and so on. Not to mention the hanging."

Lucy left Paul's office with mixed emotions. She felt buoyed by his enthusiasm, the vote of confidence in her ideas, the prospect of overcoming the block and getting back on track. Without painting, she realised, she wasn't being herself. But she was daunted by the amount of work and having to think through exactly what to produce, in quantity, even with Paul 'keeping in touch all the way', as he put it. Would she be able to deliver in the time available, would the paintings be any good?

Wrapped in her thoughts, she almost walked past the table piled with prints and cards awaiting sorting and display. They were all by Rex! She recognised his style straightaway. Had they been there when she came in? She felt a rush of excitement. And then Paul said, "Yes. Rex Monday. A talented artist. You've met him, of course. He's coming in for a chat next week when he's back from the States."

Lucy rushed from the gallery, almost forgetting to say goodbye to Paul, and made her way to the square a short distance away. She found herself in the garden in the middle and sat on a bench, barely conscious of her surroundings or of other people milling or playing or talking nearby. Around the bench, pigeons pecked and crooned, apparently oblivious to her, to how she was feeling. She shooed them away half-heartedly. At least, she thought, they're not wretched doves.

Why hadn't she heard from him? Or, more precisely, why hadn't *she* heard from him when he had apparently been in touch with Paul and was seeing him next week? He hadn't even told her when he was coming back. She had been slow to admit to herself how much she was looking forward to seeing him again.

After a while she began to breathe more evenly. She delved for her phone. Nothing. Well, she wasn't going to contact him. Where was he anyway? Still in Maine, back in New York, or what? Had she been wrong to trust him? Had he lost interest, met someone else? Had their warm words – and more – since that first night in Clapton meant nothing to him?

She got up and made her way out of the garden, wandering along one side of the square until she found a café that was not too crowded. She took a seat at a corner table and ordered coffee and a tuna sandwich. It was as much as she felt she could manage. While she was waiting, a loud chirrup from the phone that was lying ready on the table. She pounced. He was catching an evening flight from JFK, arriving at Heathrow at 7.30 am tomorrow! She felt so relieved and reproached herself for doubting him.

What time would she have to get up?

Nine

When she got home, Lucy lifted a can of fizzy lemonade from the fridge, and went to sit in the garden. She knew she should be thinking about her windows pictures but she couldn't settle – and, anyway, she was waiting to hear from Paul, wasn't she? Had it only been this morning?

She was tapped on the shoulder by a branch of the fig tree moving in the gentle breeze, as if reminding her that she had things to do. The fig had stood in its pot by the front door of her Norfolk cottage at the end of a path edged with lavender, rosemary and sage. A piece of the place she had left for good two years ago when she had begun to feel that the area inspiring her East Anglian paintings had no more for her, was beginning to hold her back. A small element of continuity as she tried to move on and a reminder too of her parents' garden in Spain. She ought to go and see them when the weather there was cooler but how to fit everything in?

After a bit, she drifted back into the house and up to her studio. The russet-covered notebook still lay on the top of the cabinet next to her work table; poking from it, the typed sheet Clare had given her, folded in half. She drew the sheet out and read it through quickly and then more slowly. She could not push away the image of the girl shut in the cupboard under the stairs, with no choice but to accept her punishment. Who was the unnamed girl, what became of her?

There were still hours of daylight and time to get through before meeting Rex at Terminal Five. Not that it would take long to walk to Brushwood Road. No need to go through the woods.

The faces of the houses she passed glowed in the late afternoon sun. The old red brick looked as warm as the day itself. The entrance to the track between numbers fifty-one and fifty-five was as rubbish-free as before. She wondered who kept it clear, cut the grass verges. She walked the few yards to where the brambles began and stared for some minutes into the thicket. It was impossible to see how far back it went, what lay beyond, whether anything remained of the lodge that Hugh had mentioned. Someone must know, surely. The results of her on-line efforts had been ambiguous at best.

She turned and made her way back to the road. Now what? She had felt impelled to come but without much idea of what to do once she got here, of how the visit would add to what she had seen the morning she had found the notebook. Hugh said the people at number fifty-one had bought part of the lodge's garden to extend their own property but that was many years ago. No one around today would remember it.

As she stood at the top of the track, a large black car drew up and stopped outside number fifty-one. Did anyone need a car that size? It looked as though it would eat her own small Fiat, rarely used.

"Can I help you?" barked the well groomed woman who wafted onto the pavement. Her tone was scarcely encouraging but Lucy bit the bullet.

"I was looking for number fifty-three."

"There is no number fifty-three. Why do you want a house that doesn't exist?"

Lucy was undaunted. "I'd heard that the number might relate to the old lodge of Brushwood Hall. The hall was demolished in the nineteenth century but the lodge may still be there at the end of the track," said Lucy, gesturing towards the brambles.

"So how do you know about it?"

"A friend interested in local history mentioned it. As there's a break in the house numbering, I wondered if number fifty-three might once have been the lodge."

The woman looked thoughtful, her manner softened, slightly. "There *is* a structure of some sort," she said. "It's close to the end of our garden but you can't see it from ground level because of the high hedge. Occasionally, we catch a glimpse of roof from the upstairs bathroom window but it's not exactly obtrusive and we rather forget it's there. No one can get to it. No problems with vandals, drug addicts, those sort of people."

"Who maintains the entrance to the track?" said Lucy.

"That's Ted at number fifty-five. A man with time on his hands. Still, I can't stand here gossiping on the pavement." The woman picked up her briefcase as if about to go into the house. "Who did you say you were? Do you live around here?"

Lucy introduced herself and mentioned the road in which she lived.

The woman said nothing for a while, apparently lost in concentration, as if trying to drag something from the back of her mind. "Not the *artist*?" she said eventually.

Lucy nodded.

"We bought one of your paintings from the exhibition at Toad Books. Must have been ten years ago, maybe more. It's in the house in Suffolk. Why don't you come in and have a drink? I'm Barbara, by the way. Barbara Wilcox."

In the kitchen cum dining room, a small boy, introduced as Henry, was doing his homework under the loose supervision of a woman presented as Marina, the au pair. Barbara offered Lucy a glass of rosé, poured one for herself, and they talked for a bit about Suffolk and Norfolk and what Lucy was doing now. Then, pausing for a top-up, they drifted through the open sliding doors into the back garden.

Barbara was becoming expansive as they 'did the tour', telling Lucy how the garden had 'had a make-over' at vast expense at the hands of a designer they had 'met at Chelsea' and who often appeared on television. Lucy had heard of him and made admiring noises at suitable intervals, wondering whether she could steer the conversation back to the lodge.

"I see what you mean about next door," she said, as they went back inside. "You can't see anything from here at all."

Any view of the lodge from the garden was obscured, as Lucy had been told, by the hedge, which was itself in front of a fence that ran along the boundary.

"Did you want to have a look from upstairs?" said Barbara. "While I find some nibbles. The bathroom's at the top of the stairs."

From the bathroom window, Lucy had an oblique view of the plot and what might have been a wedge of slate roof lurking between tight-packed sycamore. But it was hard to tell or conclude anything more than that the building must be single storey. What state it was in was anyone's guess.

"Tarallini or Bombay mix?" asked Barbara, holding out two bowls when Lucy came downstairs. "Best I can do."

Lucy took some Tarallini and said,

"I'm surprised the site hasn't been re-developed but it seems to have slipped below the radar."

"Heaven forbid," said Barbara. "The last thing we want is new development next door. Long may the place remain inaccessible. Out of sight, out of mind."

Henry looked up from the table. "I've seen it, Mummy," he said proudly. "There's a gap in the fence at the end. I squeezed through. It's the secret way that foxes use."

"When was this?" said Barbara. "You might have been cut to shreds by brambles or broken bottles or anything! The place is a tip."

"I think the building was used by spies," he said. "I found a notebook written in code."

Lucy flushed. "Do you still have it?" she asked, as calmly as she could.

"No. Marina put it in that box thing with some other books when we went for a walk in the woods. She said there was no point in keeping something I couldn't read but maybe somebody else could."

The au pair gave a vigorous nod but said nothing.

Henry Wilcox! thought Lucy. "Are your initials 'HAW', by any chance?"

Ten

Rex claimed he was suffering from jet lag. That wasn't Lucy's impression and she had no complaints! Where did he get the energy after an allegedly sleepless transatlantic flight? She disentangled herself from the sheets and eased herself up. Turning over, she glanced at the clock on the bedside cabinet. 13:14 hours, Clapton time. How did it get to be so late? They'd arrived back from Heathrow hours ago. No matter; right now there was nowhere else she would rather be.

Rex surfaced slowly, his dark hair tousled. He yawned and said, "I'm afraid there's no food in the house. I let stocks run down before I went away."

He suggested going to a newly opened crêperie for lunch. It was called Le Poisson Rouge, he said, although no fish of any sort featured on the menu.

Once dressed, they walked slowly to the restaurant a few streets away, a freshly fitted frontage between a newsagent and a hairdressers. As they made their way to a table, music from the soundtrack of *Amélie* was playing softly in the background.

"One of my favourite films," said Rex.

"Mine too," said Lucy.

When they had ordered galettes and a bottle of cider, Rex told her he'd visited the New Romulus Gallery when he was in New York and met Caroline Buffo. She ran the place, as Lucy knew, since it was the gallery that had shown her East Anglian pictures some years ago and sold the lot.

"How was she?"

"Glossy but distracted," said Rex. "She's in the throes of moving the gallery round the corner. She sends her love, by the way. I mentioned that you were working on a new series of 'windows' paintings. Jumping the gun a bit, perhaps, but Caroline was enthusiastic and said she might get in contact with Paul. I'd better warn him when I see him."

'Jumping the gun' was putting it mildly, Lucy thought, but she was touched that he had thought to mention her work. He still didn't say much about his own. Nor had he shown her his studio ('A bit chaotic at the moment!') even when she had asked, had said she'd seen some of his prints and cards at Bainbridge and Murray. She felt she needed to tread carefully, not press too hard, without quite knowing why. What did he keep in there?

"By the way, Caroline Buffo has agreed to take some of my stuff," Rex said diffidently, pouring each of them a cup of cider. "We'll have to see how they fare." Lucy was proposing a celebratory toast to the success of his work when the galettes arrived.

★

While they were waiting for coffee later, Rex bent down and pulled from his bag a soft toy in the form of a bright red lobster.

"All the way from Portland, Maine." He gently tickled her nose with its whiskers. She laughed and gave him a kiss.

"Thank you," she said, dabbing her eyes with the sleeve of her blouse. "Sorry to be so silly."

"Silly is good," he said. "There's never enough of it."

He put his arm round her and she leant in to his shoulder. They stayed like that until the coffee came and the lobster was moved to one side.

A few minutes later, Rex delved into his bag again, producing a dark blue box which he gave to Lucy.

"A little something from New York," he said. He was looking anxious. "I hope you like it."

She gasped with surprise and delight as she opened the box to reveal a necklace of amethyst and silver.

"It's lovely," she said, carefully removing the necklace. It gleamed coolly as she turned it in the light. "And such a wonderful combination of colours."

Lucy did not often wear jewellery but this necklace was exactly right, she thought, just her sort of colours. She wanted to put it on straightaway, Rex helping with the clasp at the back. How well he knew her, what she liked. A bit unnerving in a way but comforting that he did, uplifting. And the fact that he had thought to buy it for her at all, what it said about his feelings for her, even if – or because – he tended to shy away from putting things into words.

This was when she felt it really was going to be all right, though quite what she meant by 'it' and 'all right' she wasn't sure. She was confident now that her doubts and uncertainties over the past few weeks had been misplaced. What the future held, she did not know.

As they were getting ready to leave the restaurant, the music from *Amélie* came round again. Rex surprised her by taking her hand and waltzing to the door to the accordion strains of 'La Valse d'Amélie'. They burst, laughing, onto the pavement and ambled, arm in arm, the short distance back to Rex's studio.

When Lucy opened her own studio next morning she was feeling in a more positive frame of mind than she had the last time she was there. Was it only two days ago? She went to the cupboard to the left of the fireplace and removed a wooden box. It was stained dark brown, with brass catches as shiny as they had been the day she'd put it there. The box was a present from Marion Ducasse, to celebrate the impending conclusion of Lucy's Paris exhibition. They had walked that overcast Thursday afternoon from Marion's gallery in the Place des Vosges to the shop hidden in a cobbled courtyard off a street near the Pompidou Centre.

The box contained a set of hand-made pastels. At the time, they had not fitted with the style of work she was doing and seemed much too nice to use in any event. Cometh the hour, cometh the box. She took it to the table by the window, flicked the catches and lifted the lid. The richness and intensity of the colours! The neat rows of brilliant pastel sticks slotted snug inside. And the touch and feel of them! So soft and smooth, like velvet. She was enchanted. It seemed almost criminal to disturb them.

But they'd save time – there was no need for mixing. She'd need to work quickly, though, and get it right first time. There was no scope for second thoughts once she had started on a piece. She didn't want to waste any of the precious pigment so she did some preliminary sketches in crayon to set the ball rolling. They seemed wan and lifeless in comparison with the possibilities of pastel.

She started with a small 'window', a few tentative strokes in a medium she had rarely used. As she became more confident, she became more fluent. First one drawing, then another. Bold strips and stripes of burnt orange and emerald green, lilac and pale apricot, rose pink and dove grey. She found herself departing from the sketches as the finished drawings took shape and a life of their own.

The process was tiring but exhilarating. Was she really beginning to unblock the block at last? She hardly dared think. It felt like tempting fate. But she had made a start and the prospect of the amount of work ahead of her seemed a little less daunting. She was wondering when she might get Paul's detailed suggestions and timetable for the show at his gallery when a chirrup from her phone announced the arrival of an email. It was from

Paul himself. An invitation to supper with him and Clare this evening, when he would return her portfolio and share his thoughts about preparations for the show.

"Sorry it's short notice. Hope you can make it. And Clare says she has the rest of the thing her colleague Toby was working on. Some code or other."

Eleven

Clare and Lucy adjourned to the sitting room after supper while Paul was despatched to make more coffee. His views on how and when Lucy might work up her 'windows series', as he called it, were dealt with before they ate. It all sounded feasible, if demanding, and Paul was enthusiastic about the new pastels she showed him on her phone. She was still feeling relaxed, even buoyant, when Clare produced the second sheet from a folder identical to the one she had brought last time.

Although, in the absence of Hugh, it was just the two of them this time, Clare thought it better to read what she had out loud, as she had previously, rather than simply hand the sheet over. That somehow made it more of a piece with the first instalment, she said, and gave it more immediacy. And then she began, in a measured, even tone, to read the document she held in front of her.

> *I heard the row between them after Father released me from the cupboard. And on following days too.*

Had he not known? But he was not around much before then, came back late from work, and she adopted different tactics when he was at home. All sweetness and light when he was in the room with us. If he was somewhere else, she fell back to slights and taunts, words that left no visible trace. 'No one's going to look at you,' as she snatched the lipstick I had asked to see when I stood beside her at her dressing table.

He started coming home earlier. We read together more often. I to him, him to me. Things seemed to be getting better. And then they told me I was to be sent away, to a boarding school somewhere in the West Country. I was distraught. What had I done to deserve this new punishment? Was I not wanted at all?

I ran out of the house in tears. Father found me at the end of the garden. He sat down on a tree stump and drew me gently to him. It was just big enough for two. He explained that my life at home was too restricted, that I needed to meet other people, make friends, have a 'proper', more balanced education. Could I not have these things at a day school? He said that St Cecilia's would be more of a community and provide fresh perspectives. But they would, of course, come and visit and I'd be back home for the holidays.

He never mentioned her, not once, not specifically. Neither as the real reason why I was to spend time away, nor how she would spend her own time in a largely empty house. Much later, after she died, he said she always resented the constraints she felt motherhood had imposed on her, the years of missing opportunities (unspecified) that might have come her way.

No doubt she would have said it was my fault. For stopping her doing what she wanted to do. So she tried to stop me too. Yet she was terrified of letting go, of losing control, of accepting that she could not have confined me indefinitely. She was not a well woman.

"It gets no better, does it?" said Clare, lowering the sheet and resting it on the folder. Paul, who had been standing quietly with a tray by the door while Clare was reading, came and put the coffee on a small table. He left the room without saying anything.

"At least she got away, by the sound of it," said Lucy. "Boarding school must have been a shock to the system. But a release too. I wonder what they made of her or what it was like when she came home in the holidays?"

"Odd that all this comes at the beginning of the notebook," said Clare. "What on earth does the rest of it cover?"

"Unless Toby can decode it we'll never know."

"He's done his bit, I'm afraid. He was happy to look at the opening pages as a favour but he's far too busy to work on the whole thing."

"Could he tell us – me – how to decipher it? Now that he's cracked the code."

"I'm not sure it's that easy," Clare replied. "Or that Toby would have the time to go through it. I don't think it's just a case of passing on a cipher. He said the code was far from straightforward. Not a simple question of replacing each number or symbol by a corresponding letter, for example. What corresponded with what was not consistent, even in the pages he saw; possibly reflecting when it was written, like the day of the week."

"Wouldn't comparing the coded and decoded versions of the pages we sent him provide a way in?" said Lucy. "A starting point, at least."

"I don't know," said Clare. "But, either way, it would be an enormous job – and where would it leave you?"

"And there's the small question of some pictures for an exhibition," came Paul's gentle voice from the other side of the room. Had he been listening outside the door? "Don't bite off more than you can chew."

Lucy's portfolio lay on the seat beside her as the Uber took her home. She knew Paul was right, that she had to focus on the new venture now she had a clear timetable to work to.

Clare had asked her, as she was leaving, whether she had said anything to Rex about the notebook. Lucy had not thought it worth mentioning before, not knowing where, if anywhere, it was going. She'd be seeing him, of course, but what could she say about the notebook now? There was surely nothing more she could do with it, intriguing as it was.

But it was more than intriguing. There was a life

wrapped up in it and a story. And so many unanswered questions. Perhaps Hugh might have some ideas about what to do. At the very least, she owed it to him to share the second instalment and he would like to know what she'd found out about number fifty-three.

Twelve

Lucy felt the day wearing away as she sat slumped in a garden chair. She was staring at the bundle of clouds that had drifted into view, disrupting the deep blue sky. From her low vantage point they looked as though they were caught in the topmost branches of distant trees, straining to break free and resume their scudding course.

She recognised that the priorities were her pictures and Rex; the bright red lobster he had given her had found a home on the chest of drawers in her bedroom. When she had mentioned the necklace to Clare, she had said that, although it had only been a few weeks, she was already finding it hard to imagine life without Rex: his gentle humour, his quiet affection, the support and understanding of another artist. But she knew that wasn't true. She could imagine it only too well after the empty times before. She did not want to re-live them.

So Lucy did not need further distraction, to allow herself to be knocked off course just as things were looking promising at last. But the girl in the notebook, finding out what happened to her, was like an itch she had to scratch. How to square the circle?

She had sent Hugh the second extract this morning and spoken to him on her mobile at lunchtime. He was sympathetic. He didn't like unsolved mysteries himself, he said, had always thought that loose ends were things that should be tied. But, realistically, trying to decode the rest of the notebook was a non-starter without Toby's help and might prove inconclusive in any case, raise even more questions to which they had no answers. The fact that it had been written at all suggested the girl had at least reached a point in her life from which she could look back on her troubled childhood with some sense of detachment. That was surely some comfort, he said. Even if she felt the need to put the text in code, safe from prying eyes.

"Eyes like mine," said Lucy. "Or ours."

"I didn't mean that, exactly. We don't know how long ago it was written or how long had elapsed after the events she describes. Or whose eyes she wanted to prevent from reading it at the time. But if, for the sake of argument, you confirmed who wrote it and she was still alive, she might not thank you for poking into her affairs, as it might be seen, opening old wounds."

"Drop it, you're saying."

"More like, proceed cautiously, if you still want to pursue it. Given that the notebook was first found at number fifty-three, there seems a chance, at any rate, that the author was, is, Rosemary Hartley."

"We've already tried to see her," said Lucy. "It was your idea to go to Bawson Cottage."

"Yes," said Hugh. "But that was to find out more about number fifty-three itself, having established she owned the place. It was before we knew what was actually in the notebook. We weren't going to confront her with it."

"I don't want to confront her. That makes it sound like an accusation. I only want to find out what happened."

"I know. You just need to be prepared for the possibility that she might not want to tell you, could react badly. One step at a time, would be my advice."

"Sounds like Plan A," said Lucy. "Ask her about number fifty-three and play the rest by ear."

"Exactly."

"Do you have any more meetings in that part of Sussex?"

Hugh was willing in principle to join her, he said, but, with commitments in London and other parts of the country, he was unavailable over the next few weeks. Lucy would have welcomed his moral support but she wanted to make progress.

"What's the urgency?"

"None, really. I've just got the bit between my teeth. You know how it is."

He did – and did not ask why she was doing this at all. Clare, she felt, would be less sympathetic, tell her to focus on the painting. Perhaps she might leave it a while before mentioning it to Clare. It was only a day trip anyway.

So Lucy set off by herself in the small Fiat she had hardly driven since her return from Norfolk. It was an early start and she felt apprehensive, tapping from time to time on the steering wheel, not knowing what to expect or whether she would be welcome at all. After much agonising, she had decided not to prepare the ground by writing to or ringing Rosemary Hartley on the basis that anything she could say would be inadequate and possibly counter-productive. What if Mrs Hartley was reluctant to see her, refused outright, or simply confirmed what Lucy knew about number fifty-three, leaving nothing more to be said?

It had to be face to face and out of the blue, as she had said to Hugh when he suggested leaving a letter or a note last time. That did not rule out a refusal but a personal approach seemed to Lucy more likely to get her past the front door. Assuming Mrs Hartley was at home at all. It could easily be a wasted journey. At least the previous abortive visit had given her some sense of a place previously unknown to her.

Lucy chose the direct route from the London road, avoiding the village of Downing and the climb up the crumbling track through the woods. By the time she had parked the car near the entrance to the drive of Bawson Cottage an uncertain grey morning had developed into another fine summer day.

She took stock at the garden gate, avoiding the penetrating stare of the dormers set in the roof. The property was looking tidier, better cared for. The yellowing piles of grass that had lain among the apple trees had been removed and the roses garlanding the front of the house recently deadheaded, by the look of it. She began to feel more positive.

She was making for the front door, ready to grip the badger-shaped knocker, when she noticed that the side gate, set into the wall, was slightly ajar. This augured well, she thought; last time the gate had been tight shut. She changed course, then came to a halt by the gate, suddenly overcome by nerves, like the first time she had had to speak in public. It's too late to back out now, she told herself. Deep breath.

Lucy took a few tentative steps into the garden. The area by the gate was shaded by a large fuchsia bush, its red and purple flowers dangling provocatively in front of her. Ahead, a sunnier part and a conservatory clinging to the side of the house.

"Ah there you are," came a woman's voice from the direction of the house. It was brisk, business-like, but not unfriendly. "Leave the gate. I've kept it open for George. Come along, girl; no need to hover. I'm in the conservatory."

Lucy came closer. Through the doors she could see a woman with grey-white hair sitting at a table, surrounded by pots of geraniums in bloom. For a brief moment she was reminded of the woman on the cover of *Mrs Palfrey*, as if the picture had come to life. It was not, though, a quiet beige skirt behind the table but a pair of legs in vibrant leopard-print trousers.

"Don't step on the dome of St Paul's. I've dropped

the piece somewhere. I like to do a jigsaw on a Friday. It's Wren's City Churches this week."

The woman looked up and smiled broadly. "I thought you'd be back. Is the other one with you? The man."

Lucy gulped and shook her head.

"Mrs Hartley?"

"Indeed. And you are?"

Lucy introduced herself and was directed to a wicker chair shaped like a peacock's tail on full display. She bent down and retrieved a jigsaw piece and placed it on the corner of the table.

"I don't get many visitors so I tend to remember those who make the effort. This is not the sort of place for passing trade. I'm sorry, I couldn't get to the door last time. Can I tempt you to some coffee and a flapjack?"

She eased herself up, using the table for support. She motioned Lucy to stay where she was. As she made for the French windows and the gloomy interior, she stopped and turned and said, "My name's Rosemary, but you probably know that."

"Well," said Rosemary, draining her cup and putting it down with a clatter. Of her flapjack, only crumbs remained. "You didn't come all this way – from London, did you say? – to pass the time of day with a stranger. Particularly as you've done it twice. So what brings you? I hope it's worth your while."

Lucy explained about the missing house and the track choked with brambles and the lodge thought to be hidden there.

"It all seemed rather intriguing. Hugh, the man you saw with me before, found out that the place was occupied years ago by a Gordon Hartley and that it now belongs to you. So we wondered whether there was anything you could tell us."

Rosemary stared into space for what seemed to Lucy an inordinate length of time. She was wondering whether to say something when Rosemary said quietly, "I think we should adjourn to the sitting room."

Lucy took in a beamed ceiling, leaded lights, a large brick fireplace, rugs on floorboards pitted and polished by years of use. And pictures, many pictures. She'd have liked to have had a closer look but she did catch sight, to the left of the fireplace, of a Piper lithograph of a church and a drawing of a clown, which was surely the work of Laura Knight. What else did Mrs Hartley have on the walls of Bawson Cottage? This was not the moment to ask. Rosemary bent to switch on an oriental lamp and sank to a sofa, gesturing Lucy to take a place on the other one, set at right angles.

"My late husband's family owned Brushwood Hall, used to live there, until they sold house and land for development well over a century ago. But they kept the lodge. Whether for sentimental reasons or because it was an odd bit of land difficult for the builder to develop, I don't know. These days developers seem to squeeze new houses into the most unpromising sites. The family moved to Sussex, to Hopley Manor, not so far from here. But certain members – the men, of course – found it convenient to use the lodge as a pied à terre or bolthole from time to time in a part of London that was relatively out of the way. Gordon used it occasionally, to my knowledge; maybe more often. Sometimes I went with him, sometimes I went by myself. That was much later, of course."

"Was it known as number fifty-three?" asked Lucy.

"I suppose so. It never really seemed to matter. Not to me."

"But it was still readily accessible from Brushwood Road?"

"Oh yes. And someone was paid to keep the garden and pathways clear. Nothing elaborate. More a case of keeping the weeds down."

"And your husband…"

"Died many years ago. A quarter of a century or more." Rosemary paused. "An accident."

"I'm sorry," said Lucy.

"Don't be," said Rosemary, with an unexpected flash of vehemence. "I mean, time is a great healer and it was a long time ago."

"You kept the lodge on?"

"That makes it sound like a deliberate decision. We had been living at Bawson Cottage for years and I simply stopped going after Gordon died, not that I had ever been a frequent visitor. I can't say that I miss it. It was pokey and damp: one-bedroom, a sitting room and what passed for a kitchen. I did nothing about the lodge one way or the other and whatever arrangements he had made for its upkeep must have fallen away."

"So the brambles and foxes took over?"

"Looking after the garden here was pretty much a full-time job. It was rather fine in those days," she said distantly. "Open to the public. Not now."

The silence hung heavy between them for a while. Rosemary seemed to be tiring and Lucy could think of nothing to say. She was biding her time on the notebook. Perhaps later, she told herself, perhaps not at all. Then Rosemary said, "Why not come and have a look? The views at least are as good as ever they were."

They went out through the conservatory, past a raised pond from which a few white water lilies raised their heads shyly.

"Morning, George," said Rosemary. Lucy turned to see a pheasant hurrying towards the side gate. Was it the one she and Hugh had seen at the front last time?

"Remarkably tame and a small comfort to me. Looks after himself and doesn't have to be taken for a walk. Unlike the dogs of yore."

They went slowly past well stocked beds, Lucy's internal camera snapping images that appealed, might come in useful later: a profusion of apricot roses, wine-red clematis scrambling through, lording it above a mass of lavender; the grey-green leaves of more geraniums, spilling from old terracotta pots; the gothic windows of a peeling summer house, reflecting the deepening sky.

Rosemary paused to catch her breath.

"The walled garden," she said, pointing through an empty archway. The entrance was barred by a rusty wheelbarrow. There was not much that Lucy could see beyond what looked like fruit trees and the glint of glasshouses long fallen into disuse.

"I weary of bletting my medlars," said Rosemary. "I fear the days of making jelly may soon be behind me. Quince, crab apple – and medlar. Heigh ho."

"The garden's lovely," said Lucy. "But you can't do it all by yourself."

"Bob Fescue comes up from the village. He requires supervision but I couldn't do without him. His sister runs the shop."

'*Rosemary Hartley! Well, good luck with that.*' Lucy remembered the words of the sun-tanned woman and suppressed a smile.

"Dangerous places, gardens," said Rosemary suddenly. "Things look pretty benign on a day like this. Slippery steps, pointed sticks, sharp tools, poisonous plants. It pays to be vigilant."

They made it to the end of the garden and sat together on the bench that overlooked a valley in which some strands of mist still lingered. On the other side, Lucy could make out a group of pale blue beehives, taking shelter under the trees. Apple trees, she thought, bright spots of red against a background of green. Perhaps Worcesters, like they had grown at home, long before her parents moved to Spain.

"You can just see the tower of St Martin's. Over there," Rosemary said, pointing to the left. "The church has a fine stained-glass window installed only a few years ago. A *modern* design, by a Frenchman. Jean-Claude

Something. The colours are remarkable when the sun shines through. Brings the whole place to life."

"I shall make you a sandwich," said Rosemary later, when they were back in the conservatory. "A flapjack will not sustain you."

As Rosemary disappeared in the direction of the kitchen, Lucy looked at her watch. She had lost all track of time. It seemed to have stood still from the moment she came through the garden gate. One o'clock! Nearly three hours had passed. From her point of view, there was no pressing need to leave. The days were still long and it was ages before she was meeting Rex. But she was still uncertain how best to play things with Rosemary. There was no obvious peg on which to hang the questions she really wanted to ask.

A footfall and the tinkling of glasses. Lucy was jolted from her thoughts by the return of Rosemary bearing a tray.

"I hope ham sandwiches and home-made lemonade will keep the wolf from the door. Now, tell me," she said, as they settled down to eat. "The man you came with before – Hugh, didn't you say – is he anyone special? To you, I mean."

Lucy flushed. "No, no. Just a friend. A good one; I've known him for twenty years. We used to be neighbours."

"I see," said Rosemary. "And is there…?"

"He's called Rex. Another artist."

"You're an artist? Should I know your work?"

Lucy found herself telling Rosemary about her

painting, its various phases, and her current efforts to overcome the block that had blighted the last few months. Rosemary, she reflected, had turned the tables but seemed genuinely interested. And building up some capital might be no bad thing, stand her in better stead.

"Windows, you say. Is that looking out or looking in?"

"Neither, really. It's not about views through but the shapes and sizes of the windows themselves and the colours I choose to depict them."

"Are we talking about real windows or imaginary ones?"

"Both. That's to say, a real window may be the starting point for a particular painting but then my imagination takes over. So it ends up as something different."

"No women gazing longingly from rooms they cannot leave? A caged bird in the background to rub the point in?"

"No," said Lucy. "I don't do people."

"Any reason? I noticed that you didn't mention portraits among your work."

"I haven't got the skill or the patience or the stamina. Think of all those sittings. And the pressure, the expectation that I would produce an acceptable likeness. Something that satisfied the sitter and anyone else who cared. I wouldn't feel in control. Supposing they hated how I saw them, what I saw *in* them. If I revealed some inner qualities that clashed with the way they saw themselves or which they wanted to keep hidden. I'd have to be honest; I couldn't flatter for the sake of an easy life. It's too much of a risk for both parties. It's easier to take liberties with places and things than with people."

"Spoken from the heart," said Rosemary. "Sounds as though you've been down that road at some point, still bear the scars. But surely there are many ways to skin a cat, many ways to approach a portrait. It doesn't have to be a big production number, does it? A quick sketch could be just as effective, possibly more so for being spontaneous."

Where was this leading? Lucy certainly didn't feel in control now. Perhaps, she thought, honesty *was* the best policy. She should say why she was really here and have done with it.

Rosemary, no doubt sensing that Lucy needed a moment to herself, rose and said something about tea as she went into the house.

It's now or never, Lucy decided. 'If you don't ask, you don't get', as her mother used to tell her as a child. What was there to lose? At worst, a rapid and uncomfortable exit but if she kept quiet she'd be no further forward anyway. She felt in her bag and took out the notebook, ready for Rosemary's return. But she wouldn't mention that she knew what some of it said, not to begin with anyway. Perhaps Rosemary would be able to decode it herself.

"Coffee and walnut," said Rosemary, setting down a slice of cake next to the tea. What with that and flapjacks, thought Lucy, she seemed to do a lot of home baking for someone who lived by herself and said she had few visitors. Not to mention the lemonade. Perhaps Bob Fescue, the gardener, was a beneficiary.

"I forgot to mention," said Lucy, trying to sound casual, "that we found this at the lodge." She passed over the notebook and sat back.

"*We?*" said Rosemary, stiffening perceptibly. Did Lucy imagine a momentary look of panic, of concern that she had discovered something of the notebook's secrets?

"The son of the family who live next door at number fifty-one. He mentioned it when I was there trying to find out a bit more about the lodge. Apparently, he got through a gap in the fence, said he thought the notebook was to do with spies as it seems to be written in some sort of code. But he couldn't read it, of course, and the novelty wore off."

"And he gave it to you?"

"He didn't want to keep it and I wondered if it might mean anything to you."

"What about this writing in purple?"

"I think that was the boy who found it. The rest looks much older."

"And so it is," said Rosemary. "And so it is." She leafed through the notebook slowly, silently. Whether she was deciphering the code as she went or recalling what it said, reliving those childhood moments, Lucy could not tell and could not ask.

"I've not seen this in many years," said Rosemary. "I realised that I must have left it at the lodge but after a while it ceased to matter. Nobody else would be able to read it. It was the writing of it that was important to me. At the time."

She sighed and softened. A half-smile crept onto her face. "Spies, eh! That's a good one. Thank you for bringing my notebook. I don't think I'm quite ready to say more about it. I'm sorry if that's a disappointment. I was not expecting to see it and I need a little time to gather my thoughts."

She has a point, Lucy conceded. She had no warning about the notebook. It leaves things open-ended but she's not saying no. Unless this is her way of saying it without saying it. Saving my blushes.

"I've had an idea," said Rosemary. "When I'm ready, why don't you come back with your paints or pastels or whatever and do my portrait while I spill the beans? If you can spare the time. Another journey for you, I'm afraid. And for me too, in a way. Deal?"

"Deal," said Lucy, holding out her hand.

Thirteen

"You're going to do her portrait," said Rex. "That's great but what about your work on the windows pictures?" He paused and added gently. "I'm just a bit worried you're taking on too much."

They were sitting at a table at the Hi-Hat, the jazz club in Dalston they had been to after the anniversary party at Bainbridge and Murray. The first set was starting shortly so Rex nipped to the bar and came back with two large glasses of white wine. Lucy had thought it best to fill Rex in about the notebook, much on the lines of the edited version she had given Rosemary. After all, Clare, Hugh and even Paul were aware of her interest in it to a greater or lesser extent. But she made no mention of what little she knew of the notebook's contents; there seemed no point when Rosemary herself was due to 'spill the beans', as she put it.

"It was her idea," said Lucy. "She wants to re-read the notebook, get her ducks in a row, before she says whatever it is she wants to say. And, in exchange, I do her portrait."

"While you're listening to her talking?"

"That's what I assumed. I'm a woman; I can do two things at once!"

"And she knows you're not a portrait painter?"

"I was at pains to tell her but she seemed unconcerned. I think she wants to know what I see; not just her external appearance but her character, bringing out what's inside. Though I'm not sure why."

"Perhaps you'll find out when you go back," said Rex. "Would it be an idea to get some practice in first, if you've got time? Not that I doubt you'll do an excellent job," he added, smiling broadly.

The lights came up on stage and down in the body of the club as a man dressed entirely in black came to the microphone and introduced the Ray Spooner Quartet. Tealights on tables flickered in the half-dark bathing faces a warm soft gold. Lucy looked at Rex for a few moments while they listened to the band's first number.

She knew he was right to be sceptical, despite the supportive noises. She had not done a portrait in years. Why had she agreed so readily to do something she had no confidence she could deliver? It could turn out to be a disaster, not that Rosemary was under any obligation to accept or keep her portrait. She was not paying for it. But Lucy did not want to let her down, felt duty-bound to make a decent fist of the thing. She sensed it was important for reasons she could not articulate, perhaps because Rosemary's own motives in commissioning the portrait from her were not as clear as she had suggested to Rex.

How long would she have to wait to hear from Rosemary? Should she prompt her after, what, a fortnight, a month? Supposing Rosemary had a change of heart, found on revisiting the notebook that the memories it unlocked were too troubling to share? Or had simply forgotten how to decode it. But if Lucy heard no more, she would have visited Bawson Cottage at any rate, met Rosemary, put a face to the name, and brought back images and ideas which she could use in her windows paintings, not least the gothic shapes of the summer house and the tracery of her imagination.

The following evening, Lucy was sitting in the garden. It was still warm and neither light nor dark but somewhere between the two. She liked the between times, as she called them, the hours before the crisp clarity of day and the enveloping darkness of night. Dawn and dusk, the ambiguity of them, neither one thing nor the other but with qualities of their own. If the first blush of dawn held the promise of a new day, twilight, she felt, had the greater magic, the greater mystery, as colour and form receded. The garden was briefly bathed in soft blue light before being lost to shadow.

She went over again what had happened that morning. She had been getting ready to come home from Clapton, already later than she had intended, when she heard a crash from Rex's studio. She had still not been in it, Rex continuing to maintain that it was a mess and there was nothing to see. If she felt a little resentful at being excluded, she did not press, but her immediate concern was that something had happened to him. She had rushed downstairs and pushed open the door to the studio, to find Rex on his knees picking up the contents of a wooden box of tools that had apparently fallen to the floor.

"I heard the noise; I thought you might be hurt," she said, relieved that he was all right.

"Just clumsy," he said sheepishly. "I caught the box with my elbow. It was too close to the edge." He eased himself up and put an arm round her. "Thank you for coming to see. No ambulance required!" He did not appear to be annoyed or disconcerted by her sudden intrusion. On the contrary, he seemed touched by her concern.

She looked slowly about the room. There was a lot of stuff: drawing table, plan chests, filing cabinets, a printing press, and all the paraphernalia of a working artist. But far from being chaotic, everything looked neat, tidy, organised, putting even her own small studio to shame. On the walls, some of his own engravings, linocuts and woodcuts – and several more by others. She recognised work by John Nash, Charles Tunnicliffe, Edward Bawden, Eric Ravilious. And hanging by his drawing table, two small paintings. A pair of her own East Anglian pictures!

"How long have you had those?" she gasped. "You've never mentioned them."

"My guilty secret," said Rex, following Lucy's gaze. "Sometimes it's easier to be found out than to say, isn't it? No tea towels or fridge magnets, though. Let's have some coffee before you go."

In the sitting room, he said that he had long admired her work and was really pleased by her success. He was rather in awe of her, felt she was the better artist, and her work was much more vibrant and imaginative. He spent time in a largely monochrome world, constrained, trying to give expression to the words of others, illustrating books to deadlines which he often struggled to meet.

"That's nonsense," she protested. "You're a successful artist in your own right and much in demand. I could never do what you do. I just don't have the patience or the discipline. Or the skill. Anyway, I've been blocked for months, ground to a complete halt."

"But you're working your way out of it. The windows paintings are an inspired idea, full of possibilities."

It was dark in the garden now. Time to go in. What Rex had said, did that fully explain why he always seemed so reticent about his own work when he was with her – and reluctant to let her see his studio? But it was touching that he had two of her pictures and had been embarrassed to say so. Another artist in need of support and reassurance!

Fourteen

She was making good progress, she said to Clare a few days later. They were having lunch at Benchers wine bar, a less relaxed occasion than usual as Clare had an unexpected conference at two o'clock. Clare nevertheless let Lucy burble for a while about how the paintings were beginning to take on a life of their own with only a nudge, it seemed, from the artist herself. One just finished, a combination of teal, yellow ochre, mid-grey and a suspicion of burnt orange; another predominantly russet and steel-blue, with hints of violet and willow green. In some, the windows were the barest outline, little more than a suggestion; in others, frames and shapes were more readily apparent.

"Russet," said Clare. "Like the notebook! A little bird told me that you were going to try and see the woman who owned it."

Hugh! thought Lucy. "I have and she's invited me to go back when she's read it, refreshed her memory. I gave the notebook to her; there was no point in keeping the thing. Only she knows what it says."

"Why should she choose to tell you, I wonder? Given what we know of its contents. It's hardly a happy story."

"She wants to say something, though she can't go through everything, I imagine. I mean, she'd have to be selective. And we don't know how far the little we've read is in keeping with what the rest of the document says or how much ground it covers anyway."

"And she wants to do this on the basis of a single meeting," said Clare. "She obviously feels comfortable about it, with you, but what exactly does she get out of the process?"

"Apart from giving her the opportunity of getting whatever it is off her chest, I agreed to do her portrait."

Clare put down her fork and reached for a glass of water. She took a couple of sips and said,

"When did you last do a portrait?"

"Not for a while," said Lucy. "Not for a long while, actually. Not since…"

"Not since when?"

"I was going to say 'art school'," she said hastily. "That was nearly thirty years ago."

"And yet, Miss Potter, you agreed, at the drop of a hat, to do a portrait of someone you had never met before."

"She asked me and I could hardly refuse when she wanted to have me back. Call it the price of finding out what happened to that girl."

"She grew up and lives in Sussex. What's she like, by the way?"

Lucy paused. "Superficially, robust, forthright in

the way of people that sort of age. Like my parents! Regarded as a bit of a character locally, I suspect. When she ventures out."

"And below the surface?"

"Hard to say on a first meeting. Lonely, I should think, stuck in that cottage, though she puts on a brave face. But I felt there was a sadness there, a vulnerability. I can't quite put my finger on it. Perhaps I'll get a better idea when I hear what she has to say."

"Sounds like you're going to need to get in some portrait practice PDQ. Perhaps I won't tell Paul!"

Lucy was feeling increasingly anxious about what she had agreed to take on and how unprepared she was to do it. Both Rex and Clare had, in their own ways, suggested she should try out some portraiture before she went back to Bawson Cottage. She knew they were right but she found it hard to focus, to think about how she might go about it, in the absence of any target or timetable or assurance that she would hear from Rosemary at all.

In any case, there was no one Lucy felt she could ask to spare the time to be practised on. So she found photographs in magazines, catalogues, brochures, anything with a decent headshot or more that she could use as a model. She cut or tore them out, pinned them to the cork board in her studio, stuck them to the walls. Mostly women, a few men. All years younger than Rosemary, but it was practice she needed rather than a dress rehearsal.

She tried a few using coloured pencil; it gave her a degree of fine control but she felt uncomfortable with the medium, perhaps lacked the discipline and patience for it, and the results seemed to her to be stiff and lifeless. She abandoned the effort and moved to the pastels she had been using for her windows pictures. She needed to replace some of the sticks, she realised. She fared better this time. The portraits were softer and quicker and more fluent, though she had trouble with eyes and other details. Maybe pastel pencils would give her what she needed for those.

Lucy was beginning to enjoy the process, becoming more comfortable and more confident. But she was conscious that all her efforts were still, in effect, reproductions of the work of others and their viewpoints, with any amount of airbrushing, touching up, manipulation of one sort or another. The faces, the bodies, were too perfect; polished, immobile and bland. She felt little sense of the individuals involved, of their character or personality.

That was the trouble; she was working at one remove. She knew that commissions were often done on the basis of photographs but, to her, it could never be the same as sitting with a live, three-dimensional model. Not that she had thought it would be – the exercise was always going to be second best.

And then it occurred to her that she might find on the internet a photograph – maybe more than one – of Rosemary herself. No substitute for the real thing, of course, but some practice with a picture of the right person would surely help her preparation. Hadn't Rosemary said something about opening the garden at Bawson Cottage to the public? So perhaps she might find a photo in a local newspaper or community magazine. But that was years ago, not even this century, and Rosemary herself would have been – looked – a good deal younger. If there was anything at all.

Lucy searched for 'Rosemary Hartley'. The images which came up were clearly not of the woman she wanted, at any age. She refined her search by adding 'Downing, Sussex' to see what happened. There were no associated images, just a solitary result recording the opening of the local flower show by 'Mrs Rosemary Hartley, widow of the late Gordon Hartley of Bawson Cottage'.

It had been worth a try. If she had been more on the ball, she realised, she could have taken some pictures of Rosemary herself when she agreed to do the portrait. But the suggestion had been so unexpected when she blurted out her agreement that she simply hadn't thought through what it would entail. Perhaps further research would produce further results but she was reluctant to spend more time preparing for a job she was again having doubts about herself.

In any event, she had heard not a word from Rosemary, who was probably having her own doubts about revealing the secrets of her past to a virtual stranger.

Fifteen

*L*ucy went back to her windows pictures, focussing this time on collage, or mixed media as Paul preferred to call it. She used strips of drawing paper, scraps of newspaper, odd pieces of anaglypta sliced from a roll she found in the loft. She worked them into a series of gouaches, achieving an effect that was both textured and layered, with a greater sense of depth and mystery than her pastels. She hoped they would pull viewers in, lead them to lose themselves in some interior of their own imagining.

She took photographs and sent them to Paul. They did not do the collages justice but they still seemed an advance on the samples in the portfolio she had left with him that day at the gallery. She wanted to know what he thought before doing more of them.

Afterwards, she sat in the garden with a cup of coffee. Her neck and shoulders ached. The work on her windows series, coupled with the frantic but fruitless exercise on portraits, was beginning to take a toll. She had been – was – so determined not to let people down, to prove that she could deliver as she had done in the past, and not allow pursuit of the notebook and its secrets to derail her from meeting the timetable for the exhibition and the Christmas show beforehand.

She became aware of the chirruping of her phone from inside the house. It was insistent and penetrating. Can't they call back, leave a message, whatever? She was suddenly gripped by the thought that something had happened to her parents, to Rex. Panic propelled her to the kitchen where she snatched the phone that had been vibrating on the work surface. She was too late. One missed call. And then the phone in her hand pulsed again.

"It's Rosemary Hartley. Sorry if this is a bad moment."

They agreed that Lucy should return to Bawson Cottage on the Wednesday of the following week. Rosemary apologised for not being in touch sooner, saying that she had not been ready and that 'things have taken longer than I expected'.

When the call ended, Lucy started to worry that she had not given sufficient thought to the logistics of the expedition. What would she need to take with her? She rummaged under her bed and pulled out the old easel, the portable one she used to cart around Norfolk and Suffolk. She knew that would fit in the car, as would her drawing board. But she was almost out of paper and many of the pastels had been reduced to unusable stubs. They would have to be replaced. She blenched at the likely cost.

★

She came back from the art shop near the British Museum with pads in three sizes, an assortment of soft pastels to fill the gaps in her box, and a small selection of pastel pencils for more detailed work. She had also allowed herself to be seduced by a range of iridescent pastels, colours that she had not used before, choosing gold, silver and copper to give new windows pictures an extra metallic component.

Wednesday arrived and Lucy set off early. She was unsure how long she would need to do Rosemary's portrait, how long Rosemary herself would need to say what she had to say. She made good time and parked in the drive, as close to the cottage as the small white van already parked there would allow. Another visitor? She wasn't reckoning on an audience and did not want one. She struggled through the garden gate with her easel and a large canvas bag containing everything else. The side gate in the wall was open like last time and she bumped her way towards it, wondering if George the pheasant would make another appearance. As she reached the gate, an unseen voice bellowed,

"She's here, Mrs H."

Lucy jumped but recovered quickly, taking in a large red-faced man loitering on the threshold. He was wearing a white tee shirt and ash-grey jogging pants, the former pristine and tight, the latter baggy and conspicuously stained. He acknowledged her with a nod and held out a hand for her canvas bag. She followed him to the conservatory, where he deposited the bag and left with a low-level wave.

"That was Bob Fescue; the gardener," said Rosemary, entering with coffee and flapjacks on a tray. "I put him on sentry duty. I'd forgotten he was coming today but he's back working in the walled garden. He won't disturb us."

Lucy sensed that Rosemary was as apprehensive as she was beneath the lightness of the opening exchanges. Neither of them knew quite what to expect from the other. Then Rosemary suddenly snapped to and said. "I thought we'd stay in here, if that suits."

It did; Rosemary sitting in the Lloyd Loom chair with geraniums stage left, like Mrs Palfrey.

"How do you want me?"

Good point. Why hadn't Lucy thought of that earlier? A full-length portrait would be more time consuming and perhaps put her too far from the sitter to engage properly with whatever she had to say. On the other hand, head or head and shoulders might be a bit too close for comfort. She decided on three-quarter length, with Rosemary's pink linen shirt to the fore.

"Remember: warts and all!" said Rosemary, as Lucy was setting up the easel on the uneven brick floor and adjusting its height to the stool that Rosemary had provided.

"I see no warts," said Lucy.

"Who said they were on the outside?"

They maintained a silence for the first few minutes.

Lucy proceeded cautiously, conscious that with pastels there was no going back. She had to get it right first time. How long would it take, how long did she have?

She made a preliminary sketch, tentative strokes as she tried to get the measure of what she had to do. She focussed on outline and overall shape, mapping out, creating structure, fixing the rough positions of eyes, nose and mouth. Rosemary sat impassive in her chair, apparently miles away. When is she going to start talking, thought Lucy? There was no sign of the notebook so using it as a prop, referring to it as she went along, did not seem to be what she had in mind. And would she, Lucy, really be able to concentrate on the job in hand once Rosemary began, became more animated, despite what she had said to Rex?

"It brought things back," said Rosemary, suddenly. She looked and sounded distant, here but not here. "Things I thought I had left behind, firmly in the past where they belonged. If they belonged anywhere." She spoke softly and without rancour. There was no hint that she blamed Lucy for producing the long-lost notebook, for dredging up unwelcome memories. Rosemary had, after all, honoured the agreement to meet again when she did not have to.

"For years I carried it all with me, shut away inside. Writing it down was a means of coming to terms, of cleansing, if you like. There were other distractions, of course, in the interim. Perhaps I should say, responsibilities. Husband, son. Oh yes, I have a son. And a grandson. I rarely see them. In the flesh. There's that Zoom, when I can get it to work, but it's hardly the same. Arguably worse, because it underlines the absence, the fact that they are not here. Look but don't touch – because you can't. I doubt that I shall get out to Australia now."

Rosemary shifted in her chair. Her demeanour became a little stiffer, it seemed to Lucy, observing her closely from behind the easel.

"It was some time in the late 1980s or early 1990s that I heard a programme on the radio about a woman who had written an account of her troubled childhood. She found it helped to get it out of her system. I wondered about doing the same thing. Not for publication, of course, let alone broadcast. Just for myself. I had a few false starts. Nothing I wrote quite worked so I destroyed the early drafts. I did not have sufficient uninterrupted time, could not get a decent run at it. I was doing it here at the cottage in moments when my husband was not around. It was a mistake, not least because he might have come across it, read it. That would have been unfortunate, made matters worse when it was supposed to make them better. My son had left home by then."

"The code and the lodge?" put in Lucy.

"Exactly. Sounds like belt and braces but he continued to use the lodge himself from time to time, don't forget. We went there together sometimes if we had been up to town for a play, meal afterwards, and didn't want to trek back to the cottage late at night."

Lucy wondered what his reaction would have been to

finding a notebook written in code, designed, as it might seem, to exclude him – or with the effect of doing so. Or how Rosemary herself would have explained it. But the situation probably never arose.

"The lodge became a refuge. It gave me the time and space to gather my thoughts and get them down. Sometimes I drove, sometimes I went by train, into Victoria and out again. Gordon showed little interest in my doings, beyond asking me if I had had a nice time in London and not listening to the response. He was twenty years older than me, retired, and golf was a greater attraction."

Lucy was focussing on shadows and building up skin tones. She became more relaxed and the drawing did too. Then she said,

"But how did you devise the code – and apply it when you wrote? It must have taken ages."

"I didn't devise the code. It already existed and had done for years. It was one of the girls at school, Monica Bingley. Or rather, her father. He liked to devise codes and decipher other people's. Nothing cloak and dagger. Purely as a hobby. It was no part of his work, then or during the war. If it had been, I don't imagine he would have shared the code book with his daughter. She shared it with us. We used to send each other messages, put them in each other's pigeon holes.

"Several of us played the game. That's what we called it: 'Playing the Game'. It seemed pretty daring at the time but it was only silly schoolgirl stuff to stave off the boredom outside lessons, chapel, and lacrosse. *Ursula*

Cheese has a crush on Miss Topping; we're having a séance in the common room after supper; I saw Matron in the grotto with the groundsman; Guinevere Jones put her pilchards down the lavatory. That kind of thing.

"When Monica left, the game fizzled out. But I had the book and I kept it. We had not used it in a while as we became adept at coding and decoding messages without it. So no one missed it. And when it came to writing in the notebook years later, it did not take long to get back into the swing of using the code and writing at speed without referring to the book. I have it squirrelled away."

Lucy smiled to herself. So much for a code supposedly so complex that no child could have devised it but used with ease by a handful of schoolgirls. Still, at least they'd had a code book to help them.

She turned to the detail of Rosemary's blue-grey eyes. This would require concentration and the pastel pencils. The eyes combined a softness and a steeliness that seemed to sum the sitter up but where, she wondered, was all this going? It felt like the preliminary to something else.

"It was a boarding school, I take it," said Lucy innocently.

"It was. In the West Country. I arrived at rather short notice, part way through a term. My parents must have pulled strings with the headmistress, though how I'm not sure. I did no entrance exam, not even an interview. Not a formal one; just a chat with a strange woman in one of those gloomy mansion blocks near

Westminster Cathedral. She seemed more bewildered than I was."

"Why so sudden? Weren't you expecting it?"

"For my own good, they said. They often did. I was told that I would benefit from a change of scene, from the company of other girls. I had not been to school before and had no friends of my own age. Or any age, for that matter."

"How old were you?"

"About eleven, I suppose."

"And you'd not been to school?"

"I think they call it 'home schooling' now," said Rosemary. "I can't imagine it would have met current requirements. It was all pretty hit and miss and I was left to my own devices for much of the time. But at least I could read and write and list all the counties of England and Wales. With the county towns!"

"But why the change?" said Lucy, wondering if this might be the cue for Rosemary to mention the punishments inflicted upon her. "It must have been a wrench, leaving home for the first time." The eyes were taking a long time; she couldn't get them right.

Rosemary hesitated and looked away briefly. Lucy sensed that words were being chosen with care.

"Home I did not miss, if by 'home' you mean the place I lived. It was to get me away from there that I was sent off to school. I had an isolated existence and my mother was, shall we say, a little controlling."

"But it was your parents who decided to send you?"

"It was presented as a joint decision. But it was

clearly at my father's insistence. When he realised what was going on. He had started to get back from work earlier so that I was alone less but he couldn't be there all the time."

Lucy said nothing for a while. She knew the sort of thing that Rosemary had endured but she could not say so and this was not the moment to press for details if Rosemary was not ready or willing to volunteer them.

And then, to break the silence, she asked,

"So how was school?"

"Overwhelming, at first. Turning up in my shiny new shoes long after the others had settled in, formed their first friendships, alliances. Not that these things are fixed; it's not difficult in these places to go from best friend to pariah at the drop of a hat. At least, not in those days. Girls can be cruel."

"You had a bad time?" Could it have been worse than home or just differently bad?

"It took some explaining, arriving late, well after term had started. The house mistress kept a weather eye but she would have known that singling me out, showing favouritism, as it would have been seen, would have made things worse. She gently encouraged me to join in. It was difficult to get used to company and easy to be accused of standoffishness. Some girls ignored me, others whispered loud remarks and ran away giggling. But the apple-pie beds and other indignities gradually ceased. I came to be accepted and even made a few friends. The main problem was my patchy education before I arrived – whole areas of ignorance. 'Dozy

Rosy' was one of the politer names. But I caught up – ignorance is not stupidity – and I even won prizes for reading and recitation."

"And then it was home for the holidays."

"On the school train and met at Paddington. By my father, of course. Then back to the house. The place seemed deathly quiet after weeks at school. Relations with my mother were cordial, bordering on warmth, when my father was present, less so when he was not there. No physical punishments anymore – she knew I'd tell him. She tried to undermine me in other ways – stony silences punctuated by sudden outbursts prompted by nothing at all, as far as I could see. Certainly nothing I had said or done."

"Outbursts about what?" said Lucy, starting work on Rosemary's hair with gentle strokes.

"That I was getting too big for my boots, that girls didn't need education beyond the basics, that I needn't think I would amount to anything just because I had smart friends. And so on. That became the pattern. Once or twice over the years, I was invited to stay by girls from school. It gave me an insight into what constituted normal family life. I never felt I could ask them back."

Rosemary was tiring, beginning to falter. Lucy suggested a break, adjourning to the sitting room or garden. But Rosemary said she needed to maintain momentum and asked Lucy to fetch her a glass of water from the kitchen.

"Through the sitting room, right and then left."

Lucy welcomed the opportunity to get up from the stool and stretch her legs. She glanced again at the pictures in the sitting room and lingered rather longer in the kitchen corridor. On the walls, a series of grubby marks at regular intervals, all at about head height. It looked as though they had been made by the edges or corners of picture frames, now removed. But, if so, there was no sign of them or of any hooks.

And then there was the mirror. Rectangular, with an elaborate gilt frame, the glass was neatly covered by a piece of paper, yellowed with age. Odd to keep such a lovely object in a dingy corridor. Odder still to cover the glass so that it could not be used. Lucy lifted a flap gingerly, wondering what she would find. The mirror plate was a bit tarnished at the edges but her reflection was clear enough. There was nothing, as far as she could see, to justify obscuring it. She was in two minds about asking Rosemary. Presumably, she had mirrors elsewhere in the house...

The kitchen itself was scrupulously neat and tidy. Did Rosemary have help inside the house as well as out? Lucy caught the evocative scent of beeswax as she passed a polished pine table on her way to the sink. It was one of those deep butler's sinks with brass taps and a grooved wooden draining board, similar to one she had seen in the kitchen at Pyefield Court. Two tumblers were waiting for her on the draining board. She filled both at the sink and took them back to the conservatory. Rosemary did not appear to have moved.

Lucy handed Rosemary a glass and waited beside her

while she drank as much as she wanted, while sipping a little of her own. She put the tumblers on a side table and resumed her place on the stool. She still had some way to go with Rosemary's hair before moving on to the pink linen shirt.

Rosemary showed no sign of carrying on with what she had to say, whether picking up from where she had left off or heading in some other direction. Not exactly maintaining momentum, thought Lucy. Perhaps outer calm disguised inner turmoil. But what should she do? Stay silent and get on with the portrait or offer a gentle prompt?

"So what did your mother do while you were away – and when you were back? No more home schooling, I take it."

Rosemary turned her gaze slowly towards the easel. Lucy saw her eyes narrow, her expression harden, and her body tense.

"Those days were well and truly over," she said. "My mother suddenly developed an interest in gardens, having shown none before. She read about them, looked at catalogues, visited gardens open to the public. And occasionally had ideas for our own Buckinghamshire garden. Drew up planting plans, ordered plants, then lost heart or simply changed her mind. It was usually left to my father to finish what she had barely started.

"Needless to say, what he did was never to her liking. She claimed, more than once, that he had deliberately frustrated her 'vision' by departing from the plans. He had, of course, followed them to the letter. I didn't know how or why he put up with it, with her. Years later, I asked him. But that's getting ahead."

Rosemary paused and stared at the floor for a few moments before looking up and resuming. Lucy found herself pausing in tandem, pastel in hand, while she waited.

"One day we were in the garden, my mother and I, on our way to inspect her latest project. It was during the Easter holidays and not long before I was due back at school. The weather was mild but damp, as I came to remember only too well. Without warning, she halted at the top of the steps down from the terrace and accused me of conspiring with my father to undermine her position. What position, I never knew. Screaming, invective, she seemed out of control. I was too stunned to say anything. And then she tried to slap me. After the years of meekly accepting my punishments, I defended myself. I was stronger than I used to be after all the exercise I had at school. There was a tussle and my mother slipped. She fell backwards down the steps and hit her head. Perhaps I could have been quicker in running for help.

"A tragic accident, they said afterwards, and who was I to disagree?"

Lucy herself was too stunned to say anything. Whatever came to mind seemed inadequate, banal. She stopped what she was doing with the collar of the pink shirt and put down the stick of pastel. Was Rosemary trying to tell her that it wasn't an accident? A belated confession to relieve a burden she had carried for seventy years? How could she, Lucy, carry on with the portrait of a murderer, sitting a few feet away, as if nothing had happened?

Or perhaps she was reading too much into what Rosemary had said – and it was just an accident. She recalled Rosemary's words during her first visit to the cottage. *'Dangerous places, gardens.'* A simple statement of fact, no doubt, sensible advice to take care. She had almost tripped over a hose in her own garden only the other day.

Either way, she was struck by the even, matter-of-fact tone of Rosemary's account, echoing in that respect what little she had read of the notebook. Perhaps both were intended to be cathartic in some way, as Clare had suggested about the notebook itself. Except that what was written there was for Rosemary's eyes only and here she was sharing – arguably, over-sharing – with someone else. Tainted by association, thought Lucy. Was that the expression? If Rosemary had not told anyone else in all this time, she was the first to know. Lucy felt she was being used, almost as if the burden, if such it was, had been passed to her.

Rosemary sat motionless, impassive, showing no sign or acknowledgement that she had said anything out of the ordinary or that her confession might have had an impact on Lucy herself. If she had noticed that Lucy had stopped drawing, it did not appear to faze her.

Lucy was at a loss to know what to do or say so she did nothing and remained silent, willing Rosemary to make the next move.

And then Rosemary said,

"For years, I had dreams – nightmares – of my mother lying there, contorted on the steps. There seemed for the briefest of moments to be a smile on her face, as if to say that I had not seen the last of her, that I would not shake her off so easily, that I would not forget. She was right. The memories. Triggered by small things – some seen, some heard – when you least expect them."

Lucy left it for a while and then took a gamble. "The mirror in the kitchen corridor," she said. "With the glass covered…"

"Well spotted," said Rosemary. "It used to hang in the hall of the house in Buckinghamshire. I was fond of it, the ornateness of the frame, especially the birds and fruit and flowers entwined. And then she caught me looking at them, assumed I was admiring myself in the mirror. 'Don't waste your time, girl. No one's going to look at you.' I can still hear that sneering voice, see that face behind me reflected in the glass, criticising, judging.

"I eventually inherited the mirror and a few other things. It was put away for years, wrapped in blankets. But when Gordon died I retrieved the mirror from the attic and hung it where you see it now. Out of the way but not out of the way. Less need for explanations."

This did not seem the moment to ask about the pictures removed from the corridor. Instead, Lucy said, "Just *that* mirror, I take it." She was looking at Rosemary's hair, quietly immaculate in that way of hers and now recorded in pastel in the portrait taking shape, biding its time in the conservatory. "You haven't covered all the mirrors?" not that she had seen any others.

"Of course not," said Rosemary. "Couldn't put my face on without one. Lunch?"

Sixteen

*L*ucy was directed to carry the sandwiches, already prepared and covered in cling film, from the pantry ("So much cooler on a day like this!") to the table that Bob Fescue had set up in the garden. She returned for glasses and a jug of lemonade while Rosemary busied herself with setting things out. Of Bob, there was no trace.

There was a tacit agreement between Lucy and Rosemary not to look at the work in progress as they passed through the conservatory. In fact, there was no discussion of the portrait at all. Conversation drifted to how Lucy was getting on with her windows pictures, what made her become an artist in the first place, and how her parents liked living in Spain. It was good to have a break from sitting at the easel but Lucy remained wary, uncertain how they could resume as if nothing had happened, as if Rosemary had said nothing about the circumstances of her mother's death.

Perhaps she was being too precious, over-reacting, she reflected as Rosemary went back inside to make some coffee. The air was warm, even in this shady spot, and there was no sound but the buzzing of bees attracted by the lavender nearer the house. She dismissed, as unprofessional, her initial thought of driving back to London without completing the portrait. She was here to do a job and the finishing post was in sight. She could not justify failing to fulfil her side of the bargain, abusing Rosemary's hospitality, taking the moral high ground on the basis of limited understanding of an event so long ago. Lucy could hardly accuse her of killing her mother – and what purpose would it serve? The story about the mirror just made it more difficult.

She should stick to her brief and complete a portrait that obviously meant a lot to Rosemary, although quite why remained no clearer. She realised that, in trying to come to terms with what Rosemary had said, she had not given much thought to the effect on Rosemary herself. Her apparent equanimity about the events she had described perhaps disguised a good deal more than it revealed.

The distant bell of St Martin's across the valley clanged two o'clock, as if calling her to order. Right on cue, Rosemary appeared with a small tray and suggested they carry on when they had drunk their coffee.

In the conservatory, Rosemary settled into her chair, resumed her pose, as Lucy took her place at the easel. How much more, she wondered, did Rosemary have to say, what other bombshells would she drop? She began to worry that she might finish the portrait too soon.

As Lucy reached for the stick of pastel she had been using for the collar of the pink shirt, Rosemary said,

"My biggest fear, in the months and years that followed, was that I would turn into my mother. Not in appearance – I took after my father – but becoming as bitter and frustrated as she was about her life and its limitations. With more than a suggestion that it was my fault, for preventing her from doing whatever she might otherwise have done.

"I completed my schooling, and did well enough, could have gone to university, even in the late 1950s. But I wanted to get on, do something, anything. That may have been a mistake. I should have spent longer looking, thinking about what I wanted to do. I ended up, inevitably, as a secretary. A smart firm of estate agents in Mayfair. The pay was too low to give me the independence I craved. I lived at home and commuted daily. My father and I got on well. He said that, if I wanted to find a flat or bedsit, he would pay the rent. But, despite my desperation to escape, I felt guilty about leaving him by himself, even though someone came in to cook and clean. I felt torn in two. I needn't have worried. After all, my mother's death had freed him too.

"He met a woman, a widow. She was a client of his own firm, a life assurance company I'd had no interest in joining when he'd offered to pull strings. She came to the house. Lively, kind, good-humoured – everything my mother wasn't. I was pleased for him and no one made me feel I was in the way. Perhaps she had provided solace while my mother was alive as well as in the years that followed. I've no idea. But it made me realise that I'd been so wrapped up in my own misery that I had not stopped to think what it must have been like for him. Why he put up with it.

"I asked him, in a roundabout sort of way. Not my current style, I know!" For a brief moment, Rosemary's face collapsed into a smile and her eyes sparkled. Then her expression faded to impassive and the eyes became distant again. "He just said she hadn't been like that when he married her, that she changed after I was born, that she could nevertheless 'keep up a front' when she had to. He found himself coming home later and later from work – 'staying away' – until the day he discovered how she had been treating me. He apologised for not being there more. He would never have left, he said, would never have left *me*. I don't doubt that he meant it in the best sense – I'm sure he did – any more than he meant it was my fault for being born. But it made me feel doubly responsible: for the change in my mother's behaviour and for keeping my father in what became a loveless marriage. Guilty but not charged!

"I often wondered why he didn't seek some sort of help for her. She was clearly not well. Perhaps he did, or tried to, while I was away at school, and they kept it to themselves. Or perhaps he hoped that, by sending me away, she might gradually get back to being the person he once knew. Forlorn hope, if that was his thinking. But I suspect they suffered in silence and just closed in on themselves – openness was not the order of the day. Not then. Every unhappy family is unhappy in its own way, as the man said.

"My father told me I ought to get out more, meet people my own age. Or maybe the widow put him up to it. What about the girls at work or the ones I had known at school? And, through them, meet new people. Meaning men, of course. A thrilling prospect but terrifying. I had scarcely spoken to a man, apart from my father, let alone done anything else. There was my boss at work but exchanges with him were formal and stilted. I was there for shorthand, typing, and filing and otherwise invisible.

"And then Gordon Hartley appeared on the scene. Mr Hartley! He had a meeting with my boss. I collected him from reception, took his hat and coat, made coffee, tried to concentrate on my work. Talk about film-star good looks. He affected not to notice me but I could tell that he had, dunce as I was in that department. He left it a day or two and then I received a note, in the office, asking if I would meet him for a drink after work. He said he would be waiting in his car, a silver Austin-Healey, in a street near Berkeley Square. He had the sense — or, as I assumed, the sensitivity — not to suggest meeting right outside the office where we might well have been seen.

"I suppose I should have registered that the note had no contact details, gave no option for declining the invitation other than by not turning up. But I was in too much of a pother — do people still say that? — worrying whether I was suitably dressed for wherever he was going to take me, what was expected of me, about getting home late. It was my first date.

"In retrospect, he paced things well over the coming months, very well. One step at a time. Didn't rush me. Made me feel comfortable. It was nice to feel wanted. I fell for his charm, as did my father and the widow when they eventually met him. And he seemed to offer a route to independence, to leaving home and leading my own life. How naïve I was.

"We were married. I was twenty. Far too young. But it didn't seem to matter at the time that Gordon was twice my age. His life became my life. I became the dutiful wife and gradually lost touch with who I was, what I really wanted. Not that I had had much opportunity to work it out, work them out, in the years beforehand. My own fault, no doubt. I felt as though I was locked in a cupboard again and this time my father was not there to let me out. History repeating itself; first the controlling mother, then the controlling husband. To have and to hold. He was never physically cruel. Not violent at all. It was always more subtle than that, a gradual undermining of confidence and self-belief. And still everyone else was taken in by his charm and good looks, said how lucky I was. On the face of it, I had everything.

"One day he told me we would be moving from our flat in town (it was *his* flat, of course) to a cottage in Sussex that he'd seen. Bawson Cottage. In the middle of nowhere, as it seemed, knowing no one, and with our son Clive at prep school. He was only eight. Absurdly young to be sent away but I had no say in the matter. When I protested, I was told that was what happened, as if I should have known and been prepared for it. It was Gordon's old school, needless to say. I was sent to boarding school myself, of course, but in very different circumstances. After the relationship with my own mother, I was desperate to be a good mother myself and to keep my son close. I missed him terribly."

Rosemary faltered and looked down for a few moments before resuming.

"This was the mid-1970s, years after the nearest railway line had been closed and the local station with it. He said we could easily drive to Marchant and catch the train to London from there, omitting to mention that he would be taking the car to the town himself to commute to his office during the week. Leaving me stranded.

"A lively debate ensued, as they say. I had plucked up courage and stood up to him for once. It felt rather daring, gave a boost to my confidence. He wasn't used to my sticking up for myself, may even have had a sneaking respect for the fact that I had. At any rate, he bought me a car of my own – and driving lessons to go with it. I went all over the place after I passed my test – the road to Downing was a lot better in those days."

Lucy was focussing on the final details of the portrait. Fudging and smudging here, sharping up there. She looked up and said,

"So you managed to get some independence, weren't confined to the house."

"And some fun," said Rosemary. "I was only thirty or so when we came here. I met all sorts of people while Gordon was at work! Doing the sort of things I'd like to have done before I was married. But I behaved in the holidays when our son was back from school: trips to the seaside, picnics on the downs, that kind of thing. Gordon retired in 1990 and we focussed on the garden, when he wasn't playing golf. He said it would be nice to have 'a joint project', as he put it.

"It soon became apparent that he saw himself as being in charge, with me assisting, doing the things that didn't interest him. Imposing control on the garden and trying to impose control on me. He saw nature as something to fight against, overcome, subject to his will; I preferred to work with it, get the best out of it. We reached an uneasy compromise and the results, I must admit, were pretty spectacular in their day. I think I mentioned that we used to open the garden to the public."

Rosemary paused, looked wistful. "That, at least, turned out all right. Which is more than can be said for his efforts at photography. He started on the house and garden, and then insisted on taking pictures of me. Invariably at inconvenient moments. He said I should take it as a compliment that he wanted to capture me on film. 'Capture' being the operative word. That's what it felt like. I was required to sit in front of some makeshift screen he'd set up in a spare bedroom involving sheets that he'd found. Unironed, of course. Muggins in various positions before a creased and crumpled backdrop. When the prints came back, he decided which ones to have framed. Always the least flattering ones. He told me that people never liked pictures of themselves. He put them all over the house…"

"Including the kitchen corridor," said Lucy, adding some finishing touches to a sleeve of Rosemary's pink linen shirt. She had decided not to complicate matters by including geraniums in the picture, leaving the sitter against a background of soft blue-green.

Rosemary gave a gentle nod. "It was all about him, of course. It became an obsession. When he died in 2000, I got rid of the lot."

Seventeen

*L*ucy stood up and took a few steps back to look at the picture as a whole. If a portrait was supposed to be a good likeness, a clearly recognisable physical representation, she had, she felt, done a pretty good job. What more did it say about Rosemary herself, her character, what had shaped her? Lucy found that more difficult, influenced, as she was, by what Rosemary had said, what she had revealed, as she sat patiently in the Lloyd Loom chair. Someone else coming fresh to the portrait would inevitably see it differently.

It was the eyes that held her. Soft but steely, penetrating but not intimidating, betraying more than a hint of sadness, loneliness, and years of putting on a brave face. An unwavering ambiguity, if there were such a thing, but quietly determined beneath it all.

She resumed her place at the easel and pretended to make some final adjustments. What Rosemary had told of her mother's death – or possibly not told – had prompted another thought. Lucy wanted to know and didn't want to know.

And then she said evenly, "Last time I was here, you mentioned that your husband died in an accident. I hope you weren't hurt in it."

Rosemary lifted her stare from the conservatory floor. For a moment, she did not appear to know where she was, like someone rudely interrupted from their sleep.

"What? Oh no, thank you. Though I was with him." She shifted in her chair. "We had taken the footpath down to the village. It's overgrown now but we used to go that way from time to time as a change from driving. It was fairly steep in places but, despite his age, Gordon thought nothing of it. Led the way, as usual, rushing ahead like the schoolboy he wasn't. Near the bottom, he slipped or tripped where the path crossed the river, went over the low parapet wall – no proper fencing – and ended up in the water. By the time I got there, it was too late. The water was fast flowing after recent rain and I saw him carried downstream, vainly trying to grab at overhanging willows. Rather pathetic, really. They found his body later, caught in reeds."

"You saw it happening?" Lucy said slowly, putting down the stick of pastel she had in her hand. She was struck by the matter-of-factness, offhandedness, of Rosemary's account of the death of her husband of, what, the best part of forty years. Much like the way she had spoken of the death of her mother long before.

"There was nothing I could do so I went for help at the village shop. He left me well provided for. The widow had got the house in Buckinghamshire and most of the money when my father died."

"And your son?"

"Was living in London by then. He came to see me from time to time."

"Otherwise, you had the place to yourself?"

"I missed Gordon more than I expected. The cottage was strangely quiet without him. I expected him to come through the door at any moment, complaining about something I had or hadn't done. People in the village rallied round, kept inviting me to tea, encouraged me to join things I had previously avoided – the WI, the rota for arranging flowers in the church, becoming a guide at Pyefield Court. They meant well but I preferred to keep myself to myself, at least at first, and the cottage became a retreat. They assumed it was my way of 'coping', as they put it.

"And then came the day I realised that Gordon would not be coming through the door again and that I was in control of my own life at last. Rosemary Hartley, the grieving widow? Not a bit of it! Difficult to wipe tears from dry eyes. What I felt was freedom, the relief of chains removed. Mostly, I read when not doing something in the garden. Gordon had never had any interest in reading, had no intellectual curiosity at all. For me, books had long been a means of escape, entering realms and having thoughts, sensations that were beyond his control.

"After a while, I felt the need to venture further afield. I went out and about in my car, renewed a few acquaintances. Quite a few, actually. I began to feel younger, more energetic. That's when I got the bike."

"The bike?" said Lucy. "You don't mean a *motor*bike?"

Rosemary beamed and nodded.

"It wasn't you…overtaking…when Hugh and I…?"

"'Fraid so. Just a bit of fun. A rare indulgence these days. I hope I didn't alarm you."

"No. We just couldn't think where it had come from."

"How's the portrait getting on?"

Lucy was still trying to process Rosemary's latest revelations and it took her a few moments to react to the question. She was beginning to feel that the longer she spent in Rosemary's company, the less well she knew her.

She stood up and turned the easel round, the portrait now directly in front of the sitter.

Rosemary gasped but she said nothing as she stared at the picture and continued to stare at it for ages, as it seemed to Lucy. She was beginning to feel embarrassed, uncomfortable. Didn't Rosemary like it?

And then Rosemary said, "Is that me? I mean, *really* me?"

Lucy didn't know what to say. The answer was self-evident. She saw Rosemary dab at her eyes with a sleeve and wondered what she had done.

"It's better than I could have hoped," said Rosemary. "For years I doubted who I was, had to live with images imposed by others, follow rules imposed by others. This picture was done at my own behest. It feels like an affirmation that I'm me. Call it self-validation."

"Thank you," said Lucy. "It represents the person I

see, of course, so I suppose you could say it's still the view of another, an image created by another. Though not, I hope, imposed."

"I was right to trust you."

"I'm not sure why you did," said Lucy. "I'm not a portrait painter."

"Clearly, you are. Or you should be. Why did you tell me that you don't paint people? You're not telling me this is your first?"

Lucy hesitated. She moved the stool from behind the easel and sat down. "It's been a while, a long while. I did a portrait of someone who was important to me, gave it to him as a present. He hated it. He wanted flattery, or at least something that reflected his view of himself, and did not grasp that what I saw…"

"…is what you loved."

"At the time. I destroyed the portrait and that was that. What are you going to do with yours?"

"I shall indulge myself and put it somewhere prominent," said Rosemary. "Once it's framed. I haven't decided where."

"Over the fireplace in the sitting room? And why not move that lovely mirror from the kitchen corridor, get rid of the paper that's covering it, and put it opposite your portrait? That's who you'll see reflected in the mirror, not your mother. It'll show you've won, shaken off the past."

"That's not a bad idea. It's never too late to come of age, is it? I think this calls for tea and lemon drizzle cake."

★

With Rosemary's blessing, Lucy signed the portrait and took some photos, before leaning it against the Lloyd Loom chair. She folded the easel and put the rest of her things in the canvas bag. She found it hard to believe that she'd been at the cottage for a matter of hours, hard to drive away as if the portrait had been a normal commission, a simple business transaction like any other. She wondered how to leave things, whether she would see Rosemary again. Without any obvious peg on which hang another meeting, vague promises to keep in touch felt hollow, insincere.

And then it occurred to her,

"I'll send you an invitation to the private view of my windows exhibition. It would be good to see you there. You'd be welcome to stay if that made things easier."

"Thank you," said Rosemary. "And thanks again for doing my portrait and for putting up with the maundering of a foolish fond old woman. Oh, and don't forget the church."

"The church?"

"The stained glass window I mentioned last time you were here. At this time of day it should be spectacular."

Lucy negotiated the slope down into the village with some trepidation. She would much rather have taken the easier route towards the London road and home but did not feel she could refuse. As it was, the parting had been awkward in a way that the forced breeziness on both sides tended to enhance rather than diminish.

She brought the car to a halt at the junction. The sun-tanned woman – Bob Fescue's sister, as she now knew her to be – was standing at the open door of the village shop and gazing into the street. It was as deserted as it had been the last time Lucy was here. She wondered who supported the shop, how it kept going.

Lucy turned left towards St Martin's and parked a little way past the place where Hugh had turned round when they were trying to find the road to Bawson Cottage. She walked down the lane and entered the churchyard through the lych-gate, pausing to take in the building she had glimpsed across the valley from the end of Rosemary's garden. A modest structure of stone and flint, a square tower with reassuring buttresses and crenelations above. From the outside, it had a solid, timeless quality, as if nothing ever changed.

The path she took meandered between headstones starred with lichen and brought her to a porch on the south side, overseen by ancient yews that cast a pall even on this fine afternoon. Lucy hastened through the door into the body of the church. It was simple and unadorned; the large east window beyond the altar had nothing but plain glass. It was the smaller west window that made her catch her breath. Two Gothic lights and a quatrefoil above, the stained glass brilliant in the sun that struck the front, filling the walls and floor with radiance and colour. An abstract design of no obvious religious significance, as far as Lucy could tell. The varying shapes and hues gave the illusion of movement, of being alive.

Lucy was enchanted. She stepped into a pool of rose madder, shading to garnet red, before bathing in washes of orange and yellow and gold, and thence the richer tones of blue, indigo and violet. She wished she could have been there longer to see the light change through the day, move across the floor and walls, dissolving the shapes in its path.

She fished out her phone and took some pictures. She sighed as she scrolled through the results. They were woefully inadequate. She knew she could never capture, or re-capture, the experience but they would serve as an aide-mémoire. Something to draw upon for her own windows paintings and remind her to look into the artist in the absence of any information in the church itself. 'Jean-Claude Something', Rosemary had said. She hoped she could do better than that.

She suddenly felt the need to sit down, to relax and take stock before driving back to London. It had been a long day. The hours of concentrating on the portrait, coupled with the weight and confusion of history shared, had taken a toll. How reliable, she wondered, was Rosemary's account? It probably didn't matter as long as the telling of it achieved whatever Rosemary had wanted to achieve; any qualms which she, Lucy, might have had while listening were already dwindling into insignificance.

One point, though. What Rosemary had said about Gordon – his charm, good looks, how everyone else was taken in by them – had given her a momentary scare, a flash of self-doubt. Had she been, was she being, taken in by Rex? But, as she sat in the empty church, facing the calmer view of the east window, she felt confident that she had the measure of him, that he cared about her as much as she did him. His quiet support had played an important part in recharging her batteries, giving her the confidence and motivation to get her brain back in gear, focus her energies, and tackle the work needed to prepare for an exhibition. Helping her to unblock the block. No doubt, in time, he would be less reticent about himself. She would not press, for the time being. She knew they needed to give each other space.

The jangling of keys brought her to. She turned and saw Bob Fescue. He greeted her extravagantly and explained that, as churchwarden, he had come to lock up for the day. Lucy made enthusiastic noises about the stained glass and left to go back to the car.

Eighteen

*L*ucy was slow to get going the following morning. She sat at the table in her studio, feeling drained, flat after her visit to Bawson Cottage. The months before her exhibition stretched ahead of her. Doing Rosemary's portrait had at least given her a short-term goal and she had something to show for it, even if she had left the picture itself behind. She looked again at the photos she had taken. The woman in pink staring at her with quiet dignity. She selected one and sent it to Rex, Clare and Hugh with a brief message.

She wondered who, other than Rosemary herself, would see the portrait once it had found its place on the sitting room wall. Or of what would become of it when Rosemary was no longer around. Questions, she told herself, that no regular portrait painter would bother to ask. They were just doing a job before moving on to the next commission. But this was no ordinary commission; it represented the story of a life, shared with her, and she could not unhear, unsee, what she had heard and read.

How far she could believe everything Rosemary had said yesterday, how much had not been said at all, she would probably never know. The deaths of two people close to Rosemary had given her more than a pause for thought. But both were said to be accidental and she had no real reason to doubt it. If there had been anything to hide, Rosemary need not have mentioned them. The shock, Lucy rationalised, was as much in the unexpected nature of what Rosemary had said, compounded by the close juxtaposition, in her account, of two events that, in reality, were separated by forty years or more. And if those deaths were not accidental, who could blame Rosemary given what she had had to endure. She was over eighty now; it hardly mattered after all these years.

In any case, Lucy had fulfilled her part of the bargain. She hoped that Rosemary really had got what she wanted from the portrait and the process of painting it.

'And what did you get out of it, Miss Potter?' Lucy smiled weakly as Clare's imagined voice came into her head. She stared for some while out of the window to the tops of the trees in the distance. I suppose, she conceded, it's some sort of endorsement, confirmation that I can do people after all. Or could if I wanted to. Morale-boosting, in its way. It still seemed limiting, a constraint on her imagination, her ability or preference to indulge in flights of fancy. But something to keep in reserve perhaps. She wondered too how Rex and the others would react to the photograph, sent not so much to spark comment on the portrait itself as to bring the

name Rosemary Hartley to life and the whole episode to some sort of close.

Lucy went downstairs and came back with a black binbag. She removed from the cork board, from the studio walls, all the headshots she had cut from magazines and catalogues and brochures to use as models, to give her the practice she had needed before taking on the portrait. She put everything in the bag, left it by the door, and sat back at the table. There was work to do.

She leafed through her sketchbooks, looking at preliminary drawings for her windows pictures, trying to re-adjust to the matter in hand. As she did so, she came across images and ideas which she had brought from Dawson Cottage, the gothic shapes of the summer house, colours stimulated by planting combinations and random associations in the garden. Some, of course, had already made their way to finished work now lurking in portfolios. She would have to go through those too. And then there were her experiments with the metallic pastels – gold, silver, and copper – she had bought when stocking up at the art shop before going back to see Rosemary. They seemed quite promising, made her look at things differently; there was more she felt could do with those once she put her mind to it.

So much for the visits to Sussex, doing the portrait, being distractions or diversions. They were seeping into, feeding, her other work. She must remember that when she felt guilty that she had been time-wasting, should have been focussing on other things.

Lucy thought of the stained glass she had seen at St Martin's. Was it only yesterday afternoon? She reached for her phone and looked at the photos she had taken. She was delighted by the washes of colour on the floor of the church that she could almost feel immersing her. Another promising area to explore in developing her own pictures.

'Jean-Claude Something', the artist. It took little searching on line to establish that his surname was Valmy, that he lived and worked in a village to the north of Paris, and that he had a website with many other examples of stained glass he had designed for churches and chapels and houses in France and beyond. And there were images of the windows at St Martin's, crisper and clearer than the ones on her phone and all providing inspiration for developing her own ideas.

Lucy was wondering how much to say about her time at Bawson Cottage. She had shared a photo of the finished portrait but people – Rex, Clare, Hugh – knew that Rosemary had had things to say to her, that Rosemary 'spilling the beans' was part of the deal that took her back to the cottage. She needed to decide what to keep to herself and what she should treat as having been said to her in confidence. She felt obscurely protective of Rosemary, even if Rosemary herself had not seemed unduly diffident.

In any case, she did not want to say everything three times, though each of them had a slightly different interest and level of knowledge. Unlike Clare and

Hugh, Rex had not seen the notebook entries about Rosemary's early life, although she had decided to tell him a bit about them. Only Hugh had been to the cottage, had some sense of the place, even if he had not seen inside. As she was thinking about what to do, her phone rang. It was Hugh, the first to react to the portrait.

"She looks quietly determined," he said. "Tough as old boots but with a soft centre and perhaps a hint of sadness. Or maybe I'm being influenced by what little I know of her childhood. A good person to have on your side, not so good to have against you. Either way, I think it's a wonderful picture. I hope she was pleased with it. I hope you are too."

"She seemed to be. It was important to her to have a portrait that she had commissioned herself. I don't think I made a complete hash of it."

"Far from it."

"How can you tell? You haven't met her."

"Not necessary," said Hugh. "I mean, most portraits you see on gallery walls are of people who died years ago. No one around today ever knew them. That doesn't stop us admiring a Rembrandt or a Gainsborough."

"I'm hardly in their league," said Lucy.

"Are you taking commissions?"

"No! This was strictly a one-off."

"If you want to fill people in on your time with Rosemary," said Hugh, "why don't we have everyone round for supper at Falstaff Road? I'm sure Kate would jump at the chance of meeting Rex again. Seems he made an impression at that reception in Hoxton. Leave it with me."

It was probably the simplest solution, she reflected, killing several birds with one stone. But 'everyone', she realised, meant six people, three couples: her and Rex, Clare and Paul, Hugh and Kate. She blenched at the thought of five others being present when she recounted selected highlights. It changed the nature of the thing, despite knowing everyone well. Kate and Paul were hardly in the loop at all, though Paul had probably overheard something of the second notebook extract the evening she went to supper. This was beginning to feel like a breach of trust, of Rosemary's trust in her. She'd need to give some thought to handling.

One thing just for Hugh, though.

"You remember the motorbike that overtook us on the way back from Bawson Cottage? It was Rosemary, having 'a bit of fun', as she put it. Can you believe that?"

"Only with difficulty," said Hugh. "She's in her eighties, for goodness sake. Does she make a habit of racing along the lanes of Sussex, terrorising motorists?"

"I doubt it, though she may have done once. When she needed the sense of freedom and exhilaration. She called it 'a rare indulgence' these days."

"I shall look at the portrait in a new light."

The get-together at Falstaff Road the following week was much looser, less structured than Lucy had feared. No formal reporting back, more a series of anecdotes about the time she had spent with Rosemary and some insights into what Rosemary had told of her life. She said something about the controlling natures of the mother and the husband – but not the circumstances of their deaths – and how and why the notebook came to be written in code.

"So much for Rosemary avoiding the same trap as her mother," said Clare. "Sounds as though her married life was just as unfulfilled and any early hopes came to nothing. Why did she put up with it?"

"Who knows?" said Lucy. "They were different times, she had no income of her own, and she did have a son, of course. Not that she saw him when he was away at school – and the husband spent much of the week in London."

"A lonely life," said Kate quietly.

"Yes," said Lucy, who had omitted to mention Rosemary's hints that she had something of a social life during those years when time and circumstance allowed. "You know, Rosemary's story has helped put my own temporary difficulties in perspective. How can a few months of painter's block compare with the years of abuse she endured, with so much waste of a life? I'm fortunate by comparison."

"As we all are," said Clare, with feeling. "At least some things have changed for the better."

"I promised to invite her to my private view so you may meet her then."

"I hope she lives up to the portrait," said Clare. "It's really good. It's like she's in the room with you, a powerful presence, even on the basis of a photo on a phone. I'll look at a larger version on my laptop; that should be even more striking." Paul nodded vigorously and said something about another string to her bow and longer-term possibilities – but left it at that.

Lucy was conscious that Rex, normally so relaxed and easy going, had been relatively quiet throughout the evening. He had met all the people before, would not have found them intimidating, and no one sought to exclude him from the conversation. On the contrary, they asked about his work, his trip to the States – and Paul confirmed that Rex too would be having an exhibition at the gallery some months after Lucy. So what was it?

She asked him gently as they were walking back from Falstaff Road.

"Nothing, really," he said. "I was thinking, not moping. Despite everything you've told me, and what I learnt this evening, I've never quite grasped why you pursued all this in the first place. Everyone else seemed to take it for granted."

"'All this' wasn't all this to begin with," said Lucy. "That's the thing. It was more a chapter of accidents, a series of steps, one thing leading to another. I was intrigued, drawn in, at a time when I couldn't concentrate on my own work and needed a distraction. I wanted to know why the notebook I found was written in code, what happened to the girl whose story we started to uncover, and how that missing house fitted in. I suppose I could have stopped at any point but then I would never have done the portrait. That I didn't anticipate; it came right out of the blue."

"I'm glad it did," said Rex. "It's a bloody good picture and both you and Rosemary benefitted from doing it or having it done. A score draw. But the portrait's a bit puzzling in some ways. That was the other thing about all this."

"What ways?"

He paused for a moment, then said: "There's an ambivalence about it. I'm not sure whether it's the sitter or the artist or both. Or just me. Did you – do you – actually like her?"

It was Lucy's turn to pause. "I painted what I saw and felt. She's kind and caring. I just think she needed more over the years to be kind and caring about."

They stopped outside Lucy's house in Dogberry Road. Ozymandias was in his familiar position on the front wall, purring loudly. Lucy introduced him to Rex, who rubbed the cat between his ears while she rummaged for her keys. Then she opened the door and the couple went inside.

Nineteen

*L*ucy had now completed a substantial number of windows pictures. She was pleased with her achievement, even if her pastels were worn to stubs, but the weeks of concentrated work had taken a toll. She was exhausted, desperate to escape the confines of her studio, to get out of the house entirely.

Early mists had cleared and a cold grey morning had developed into a bright autumn day. Lucy made her way to the woods and walked slowly through them, warmed by sun that penetrated the thinning canopy. She was not in a hurry but she had no wish to linger: today, the place had a quality altogether different from that of the green-gold morning of her visit in the summer.

Both Rex and Paul had told her to take a proper break. She was off in a few days to see her parents in Spain now that the weather there was cooler. Just her. She had wondered whether to ask Rex to come too but concluded, reluctantly, that meeting parents was premature. It would change the dynamics of a visit to family and she would be unable to relax, feeling that the couple were on show, under observation. In any case, Rex kept saying he was well behind with the illustrations for a new edition of the poems of John Clare and that the publisher was becoming restless. So he needed to stay in London and catch up. But he had given Lucy one of his wood engravings to present to them with his compliments. A small hedgehog snuffling among dry leaves.

"Not too sentimental, is it?" Rex had asked her.

"Yes," she had replied. "That's why they'll like it. It says a lot about you!"

Lucy left the woods by the same exit as before, a short distance from the 'little library' where she had deposited *Mrs Palfrey* and come across the russet notebook. The old metal cabinet on a pole had been replaced by a smart new box, whose bolt slid open without complaint at the touch of a finger. As far as she could remember, the books inside were all different from the ones she had seen last time and *Mrs Palfrey* was not among them. She felt a stab of loss; it was wholly illogical, she told herself. What had she expected? The book had never been hers and, with luck, it had long been back with its rightful owner. And, if not, it was no doubt being enjoyed by someone else. But she could not erase the image of the woman on the cover, staring at her, as it had seemed, almost appealing to her for help. The image that had stayed with her when she met Rosemary and set about doing her portrait. A woman in a Lloyd Loom chair surrounded by geraniums.

Lucy shut the cabinet door and decided to head for Brushwood Road, just as she had the last time she was here. If nothing else, she thought, repeating the action had an appealing symmetry, as if part of a ritual. Something she did after going for a walk in the woods. There was no mystery about the notebook anymore or its relationship with number fifty-three.

She heard the noise before she reached the place. The disturbing buzz of a strimmer, frantic, insistent. As the entrance to the track leading to number fifty-three came into view, she saw that the strimmer was wielded by a white-haired man in a lumberjack shirt. But what caught her attention was what lay at the end of the track. In place of the bramble thicket was a solid barrier, a high double-gate set into a hoarding that appeared to continue along the boundary to both sides. A sign decreed that hard hats must be worn and warned parents to keep their children away. There was no activity on site at the moment, though; the gate was padlocked shut.

What was happening to number fifty-three? Had Rosemary decided to sell up and consign the abandoned lodge to the same fate as Brushwood Hall, the building it had once served? Lucy felt obscurely resentful that she did not know. She spoke to the white-haired man, who turned out to be Ted from number fifty-five, the neighbour Barbara Wilcox had mentioned liked to maintain the entrance to the track in the interests of a tidy road. Ted confirmed that, far from squeezing a 'luxury development' onto an unsuitable site (as the neighbours had feared), the old lodge was being refurbished by the current owner; the grounds, such as they were, were to be landscaped. Ted went back inside his house and reappeared with a sheet of paper. Copies, he said, were put through letter boxes in the vicinity a fortnight or so ago.

The sheet was a single side of A4. Lucy scanned it quickly. The text confirmed what Ted had said, had a few lines about the history of the lodge and the Hall, and had photographs of both. The one of the Hall was a reproduction of an early print, in which the house was described as the *Seat of Thomas Maltby Esquire*; it was surrounded by parkland, fringed with trees. The one of the lodge was much more recent. Crisp and clear, it looked as though it might have been taken shortly before the place fell into disuse. And there were roses round the windows that reminded her of Bawson Cottage.

Ted said he'd never met the owner and nor had anyone else in Brushwood Road. The name and number at the bottom of the sheet were those of the project manager overseeing the work.

"Looks like my strimming days are numbered," he said wistfully.

Lucy took a picture of the information sheet with her phone and looked at it more carefully on her way home. The Hall itself looked Georgian; simple but elegant. The lodge was more playful but did not quite match the gingerbread-house image she had formed of it. A building she had never seen beyond dark hints of roof among the vegetation. She was glad that the lodge was to be brought back to life but she remained puzzled. What was Rosemary intending to do with it? She had hardly spoken fondly of the place: '*It was pokey and damp: one-bedroom, a sitting room and what passed for a kitchen.*'

Lucy was in her own bedroom a little later, thinking about what clothes to take with her to Spain. On the top of her chest of drawers, a bright red lobster reminded her that she would be seeing Rex this evening. And that she needed to buy sun tan lotion to avoid becoming that colour herself. As she added it to the growing list of things she still needed to do, she heard a car door slam outside. A rare enough event during the day in this quiet south London street. And then another door closed, the sound softer and more tentative. Two cars or two doors of the same car? She was crossing to the window to have a look when the doorbell rang.

In the hall, she made out two shapes through the obscured glass of the front door. Jehovah's Witnesses? Should she open the door or wait for them to go away? If it was anyone she knew they would surely have let her know they were coming. Then came a voice, one of them speaking to the other. It was unmistakeable. Rosemary!

Lucy wrenched the door open and greeted her warmly. But it was the man standing behind her that made an impression. Tall and tanned, sixtyish she reckoned, he contrived to appear both confident and sheepish. He was holding a box and looked as though he didn't want to. She had never seen him before but recognised him straightaway.

"This is my son, Clive," said Rosemary, waving airily without turning to look at him. "He's over from Australia," she added, as if in explanation for their sudden arrival on Lucy's doorstep.

Lucy took them through to the garden and settled them around a table while she went to make some tea. She found a packet of biscuits that had not gone soft, feeling the offering seriously less than adequate compared to Rosemary's conjuring of flapjacks and lemon drizzle cake at Bawson Cottage. Through the kitchen window she looked at Clive talking to his mother. Since he did not bear much resemblance to Rosemary, Lucy assumed that he must take after his father, Gordon Hartley. Which, despite Clive's years, shed some light on what Rosemary must have seen in the young Gordon and why she had said that people were seduced by his charm and good looks.

Lucy wondered how much Clive knew of Rosemary's early life, of her mother's controlling nature – and his father's, come to that – and of the circumstances of their deaths. Or perhaps his parents maintained a front for his benefit. She'd have liked another perspective but it was hardly something she could ask now, and when would she have another chance?

When Lucy appeared with a tray, Clive stood up to

help and Rosemary said they had been admiring her acer, now in its fiery red finery. After a few minutes of polite conversation, Clive said he had been keen to meet the person who had painted the portrait of his mother. She had sent him a photograph of it and then, when he came over, he saw the original on the wall in the cottage. He was softly spoken, his accent English with hints of time spent in Australia. His mother, he said, had carefully positioned an elaborate mirror on the opposite wall so that she could be seen in that too, framed by fruit and flowers, as befitted a keen gardener. "So there's no escape from her!" His tone was teasing but affectionate.

"Bob Fescue put them up," said Rosemary.

"Acting under instruction, I daresay. Anyway, the portrait looks more like my mother than she does, if you can believe that. Either in the flesh or on Zoom. Spooky or what?"

Lucy was unsure what to say. "I'm glad you like it. I enjoyed doing it. It was breaking new ground for me. I don't normally do people."

"Then you should," said Clive. "I had a look at your website. Seems you're pretty versatile."

"It goes in phases," said Lucy. "I do one thing then move on to another."

"Clive," said Rosemary, perhaps feeling the need to intervene. "The box."

He turned to the box sitting on the chair next to him and made to pick it up. Lucy could see from the lettering on the lid (*Lincoln, Bennett & Co. Ltd, Hat*

Manufacturers, 40 Piccadilly) that it was an old hat box. A cube, grubby and stained but still exuding the sense of solidity, even class, of a box as well made as the hat it must once have contained.

"I suggest you remove the lid," said Rosemary.

He put the lid on the table and Lucy saw inside the box several items enveloped in bubble wrap.

Clive eased out the first and handed it to his mother. She unwound the wrapping deftly and passed the item to Lucy.

"A few early efforts of my own," she said, as Clive took the wrapping off the others. "We had them framed. Childish things, perhaps, but some tokens to say thank you properly for my portrait."

Lucy recalled references in the notebook to Rosemary illustrating birds and plants and insects found in her parents' Buckinghamshire garden. The four pictures she was given were of plants or flowers – apple blossom, columbine, nasturtium, Japanese quince. A random selection, exquisitely captured in pencil and watercolour. Lucy was delighted and momentarily lost for words.

"These are lovely," she managed. "Thank you so much. But why did you not keep up with your painting? You have a real talent." She wondered what had happened to the others, what would happen to them 'in due course'. Would Clive value them?

"They reflect a moment in time," said Rosemary. "Life got in the way and eventually I focussed on creating gardens rather than recording them."

Lucy went back inside to make more tea, still feeling dazed by the unexpected present of Rosemary's paintings. She must show them to Paul. Not that there was any shortage of work by competent botanical artists but these had something, a certain old-world charm, perhaps, that set them apart.

And what of the unexpected arrival of Rosemary herself, with Clive in tow? Had they really made the journey from Sussex on the off-chance that she would be in? She had, of course, done much the same herself in the other direction but not with something specific to hand over. Would they have risked leaving the box on the doorstep if she had not been in? Maybe they had other reasons for being in the area.

Lucy decided to address the question directly as she put the tea tray on the table outside.

"I was walking along Brushwood Road this morning," she said, "and noticed that there was a hoarding around the site of the lodge. Someone I met told me the building was being refurbished, restored to its former glory."

"That's the plan," said Rosemary. "As a matter of fact, I was going to show Clive on the way back, not that there'll much to see at the moment, I imagine, as work has yet to begin in earnest. I came across a photograph of the place some while ago. It showed the lodge as it was in better days and could be again. It brought home to me that no one else around now had known it or would ever do so if it was simply bulldozed. Clive never went there."

"I'm glad the lodge will have another life," said Lucy. "It seems right, part of the history of the area. I was shown a photo of it on a leaflet distributed to neighbours."

"That's the photograph I found."

"What will happen to the place when the work is done?"

"It remains to be seen," said Rosemary. She looked and sounded uncomfortable, which struck Lucy as odd given her apparent equanimity in the face of revelations made at Bawson Cottage.

"There are a number of options, various possibilities. I need to give them further thought. Talk them through with Clive," she added. Clive himself said not a word, sat quietly nibbling the last remaining hobnob on the plate.

Twenty

Lucy took the pictures inside and lined them up against a wall. She took photos of each one separately and sent them, with brief messages, to Paul and to Rex. She then put them in the bubble wrap in which they had arrived with a view to thinking about where to hang them after she got back from Spain.

Her thoughts turned to Rosemary's visit. She had been different somehow, more formal. Perfectly friendly but a little stiff and not the relaxed and chatty woman she had met at the cottage. Perhaps it was the presence of Clive that had inhibited her, as if there were things she did not want to say in front of him. Did this account for her reticence about the future of the lodge?

Lucy went upstairs to finish sorting clothes on the bed before preparing to go and see Rex. They were both being chased by the gallery to deliver pictures for the Christmas show that was opening next month. Or at least the ones that would need framing. As was the tradition at Bainbridge and Murray, this show would be 'off the wall', meaning that people could take pictures when they bought them rather than wait until the end of the exhibition. That in turn meant that more pictures were needed than could be displayed at the start in order to fill the gaps it was hoped would rapidly begin to appear.

Lucy unzipped her portfolio and, for the umpteenth time, went through the pictures she was taking with her to Rex before they made a joint delivery to the gallery in the morning. She felt apprehensive. This would be the first time her windows pictures were put on public display. Pleasure, relief, at having managed to produce them in the first place, at putting the block behind her, was tempered by nagging self-doubt. Supposing nobody liked them, thought that they failed to live up to her earlier work or the work of other artists on display? How would that bode for her own exhibition next year?

Rex was enthusiastic when she showed them to him later in Clapton, told Lucy she had nothing to worry about. He felt rather ashamed, he said, that he was offering no new work himself. Instead, he had dug out some original artwork for book illustrations done years ago, together with a sheaf of engravings to re-stock the browsers.

"You know," he said, coming close and putting an arm around her. "This is not just a first outing for your windows. It's the first time our pictures will have been shown together." He seemed moved, almost tearful, which moved her too.

★

Two days later, Lucy was sitting in the shade of a sweet chestnut, feeling drowsy after an early flight to Malaga. Her father had picked her up from the airport, some twenty minutes from the house – or *finca* as her parents preferred to call it. It was a converted farmhouse and had a swimming pool. She gazed at the surface of the water, still but not still, as it glittered and flashed in the late October sun.

She put out a hand and lifted her glass of chilled lemonade from the long table that would shortly be laid for lunch. She ought to move, offer to help, but she found herself looking beyond the pool, beyond the end of the terrace, towards olive groves and the mountains in the distance. To one side, a spreading fig tree, enormous compared to the one in the garden of number thirty-six. And the abundant purple fruit, bloated and faintly obscene, put to shame the puny green specimens on her own small tree, stolen by squirrels and buried in pots and beds.

"Penny for them." This from her mother, who had come back from the supermarket in the village with peaches, anchovies and tomatoes.

"Sorry," said Lucy. "I was miles away. Is there anything…?"

"Why don't you unpack while I find your father and put him to work."

In the sitting room, Lucy paused, her eyes taking time to adjust after the bright light outside. Some of her own paintings, she saw, had been brought together from various parts of the house. They charted her career over the years, the changes of style and subject matter: the Turkish watercolours, the East Anglian paintings, the colourful abstracts. Lucy Potter in microcosm.

By the stairs, she spotted two other paintings that she had not seen before, or not for many years. Crudely painted on thick paper, torn at the edges, and now protected by clip frames. Both signed 'Lucy' in the bottom right-hand corner. She must have been, what, seven or eight, a pupil at the school in the village where they lived. Closed, she'd heard, children having to go to another school miles away. One picture showed red trees against a green sky. A rather effective use of complementary colours, Lucy thought. It had been condemned at the time as ludicrous – green sky! – by the woman charged with teaching them art. It still rankled. The other picture showed two figures, barely distinguishable but helpfully labelled 'Mummy and Daddy'. Lucy smiled. So she had done people all those years ago!

She wondered when best to give her parents the paintings she had with her now, the windows pictures that were not going to make it to the Christmas show at Bainbridge and Murray. She had brought a pair: two versions of the same picture. A daytime version, with tones of orange and yellow and beige, and a cooler nighttime depiction, comprising blues and greens and greys. She liked the contrast between them, the differences somehow underscoring what they had in common. She hoped her parents would like them too.

She turned to look at some of her father's own paintings on another wall. They were juxtaposed with a selection of works by Lionel Pybus. Her father, Raymond Potter, had been a pupil of Pybus, and lent some of his collection for the artist's retrospective in Cork Street. Seeing them again was like stepping back in time — or, rather, like time standing still. As she made her way upstairs, she wondered how long her parents would remain in the house, remain in Spain. But they seemed active enough, looked as healthy and robust as ever. They were, she realised, about ten years younger than Rosemary, who showed little sign of slowing down. Even so, she thought, and continued to think as she opened her case and began to put the contents on her bed. Among them, a small package. It was wrapped in tissue paper and cardboard but she could see it clearly in her mind's eye: an engraving of a hedgehog snuffling among dry leaves.

Lucy produced the package from her bag after they had finished the soufflé her mother had made from their own oranges and before the appearance of coffee. Her parents were as delighted by Rex's picture as Lucy had hoped and expected, her father praising the technical quality of the engraving, her mother much taken by the subject matter.

When her father was in the kitchen, her mother said: "We like Rex. That sounds odd considering we've never met him. What I mean is, we can see that he's a good thing, for you. We may be old but we're not daft."

Lucy nodded but did not look up from the table.

"Remind me how long you've known him."

"About four months." Almost to the day, she realised, since they met at the reunion. "But I knew him years ago at the art school."

"And he lives the other side of London?"

"Yes," said Lucy. "His studio is there too."

"And that arrangement works all right? One of you having to trek to the other."

"It suits us. We give each other space, have our own domains, but see each other pretty often."

Lucy was expecting a question about the longer-term, perhaps because it was one she sometimes asked herself. But if it was in prospect it was forestalled by the arrival of her father with a tray of coffee and conversation turned to other things. At least, she thought, the days of hints about grandchildren were past. Even they must have accepted that that train had left the station.

The following morning, her father sidled up as Lucy was sitting at the table near the pool. She had been peeling an orange and dividing it into the segments that now lay on the plate in front of her. He continued to look furtive, almost embarrassed, as he pulled up a chair and joined her. Her parents had been effusive about the two windows paintings she had given them last night but it seemed that he had more to say.

"Those pictures," he said. "And the other ones you shared with us on-line." He faltered momentarily. "I think they're the best work you've done, and that's saying something. You're a better painter than I ever was. I'm proud of you; we both are." He looked away, apparently finding something of greater interest on the ground.

Lucy dabbed her eyes with a napkin and used the silence by consuming a segment of orange. She was affected not just by her father's words but by his awkwardness in saying them. Praise from her father meant a lot to her, more even that from Paul or Rex, much as she valued their support.

"Thank you," she said quietly. "For a while I wondered whether I'd paint anything again."

"You'd have been miserable…"

"I was."

"Painting's what you do, what you have to do, who you are."

"I know."

"And the portrait of that woman…"

"Rosemary."

"I hope she was pleased with it."

"She seemed to be, said it validated her as a person, in a funny sort of way."

"That's painting for you, whether you're an artist or a sitter. Or just someone who sees pictures on a wall offering a view of the world."

"We'll have to see what people think of my windows paintings," said Lucy. "It's one thing to unblock the block sitting in a studio, another to expose the results to wider gaze."

Twenty-one

Lucy had been worried about the Christmas show. Concerned not simply that her own pictures would not sell – she had no idea how they would go – but that Rex should do well. She had no reason to suppose he wouldn't; it was just that she could not bear the thought of him being disappointed, knowing that he would affect to shrug it off, if he said anything at all.

In the event, her fears proved misplaced. They both sold all their pictures off the wall and many of Rex's unframed prints in browsers were snapped up too. Lucy was delighted and relieved and dared to feel that it boded well for her own show in January and Rex's later on. Arrangements for her show were now well advanced and the catalogue finalised for printing, going on-line a few days before the private view.

Rejuvenated by her trip to Spain, during which she had done little more than sit by the pool or wander into the village, Lucy had produced several more pictures when she got back and taken them to Hoxton just in time. Each was inspired by the stained glass windows of

St Martin's, the light washing through them. A version rather than a representation, she said.

So now she had a breathing space. It gave her time to focus on the new picture she had started. The experience of doing Rosemary's portrait, and the positive reaction to it, had given her the confidence to contemplate doing one of Rex. Just head and shoulders. She sat at the easel in her studio, a new set of pastels to hand. From time to time, she glanced at the photograph displayed on the laptop she had placed on the cabinet next to her work table. It was in the space once occupied by a russet notebook.

The work she had done from photographs in magazines to prepare her for embarking on Rosemary's portrait had persuaded her that drawing from life was the only satisfactory way of doing it. Using photographs as an exercise was fine, but not more than that. This was different, though. She knew Rex quite well enough to bring out the nuances of character and appearance that the laptop picture did not capture. And, since it was supposed to be a surprise present, she could not very well have asked him to sit for her. He would almost certainly have declined anyway, praying work commitments in aid. He was, as she well knew, much more diffident and self-effacing, and less self-confident, than his one-time reputation as a womaniser would have suggested.

It was the week after Christmas. Paul had invited Lucy to the gallery to see how the work of hanging her pictures was going, though she had already approved the broad arrangement and this was reflected in the catalogue.

"The walls are very white," she said, as she walked around the exhibition space.

"They are," said Paul good-humouredly. "As they have been since the place opened."

"I know. But they seem a bit stark, clinical. They make the pictures stand out, as something other, if you see what I mean. Objects on a wall, pushing you away rather than drawing you in."

"I don't think you need worry. The white walls help to put the focus on the paintings rather than competing with them. We just try to hang them to their best advantage."

"You're right, of course," said Lucy. "It didn't seem to matter with my exhibitions at Cork Street, where the layout was different. Or with the Christmas show last month. Everything was faster moving, more like a market, and there was a much bigger variety of pictures. I suppose mine don't look so bad really."

"They're looking very good. I've had quite a bit of interest on the back of the Christmas show. The private view should be packed what with your list, my list, and the usual hangers-on. Come and have a look at the poster."

Paul took Lucy through to his office. He unrolled a tube of paper that was lying on his desk and fixed it with magnets to a metal board on the wall.

"What do you think?"

She took in the words:

WINDOWS
New Paintings
by
LUCY POTTER

They were superimposed on a blown-up detail of one of her gothic windows, inspired by the summerhouse in Rosemary's garden. The words picked out some of the colours in the picture.

Lucy was overwhelmed. Seeing her name in bold, bright letters on that A2 sheet was a kind of vote of confidence: confirmation that, after all the efforts, the doubts, the uncertainties of months, she was really back and had succeeded in entering a new creative phase.

"It's lovely," was as much as she could say.

"I'll send you one," said Paul, "together with a batch of the flyers and a copy of the catalogue. It's not too early for a glass of champagne, is it?"

Lucy felt light-headed when she arrived at Rex's studio in Clapton later that afternoon. She was beginning to feel that it had been unwise to celebrate her forthcoming exhibition before it had opened, before they had even finished hanging the pictures. Her initial euphoria at seeing the poster was wearing off.

"It's tempting fate," she said to Rex. "And the nicer Paul is to me, tries to humour me, the more I feel he must be softening me up, preparing me for the worst. And all those people coming."

"It's just first night nerves," said Rex.

"Before the first night?"

"You heard what people said about your pictures that evening at the Christmas show. And then they bought them."

Lucy curled herself up small on the sofa while Rex put on some jazz and went to the kitchen to make her some coffee. She looked up when he was back with a mug and said,

"I see Two Rexes! Rex Monday in stereo."

She had given him the portrait when they were together at her house on Christmas Day. She had panicked the night before that he wouldn't like it, that it would suffer the same fate as that other portrait years ago. It was hated by the man she gave it to and she had destroyed it. But Rex had been bowled over, not just by the picture itself and the evident care and skill with which it had been done but by the thought behind it. The fact that she had done it at all.

He looked confused for a moment as he handed her the coffee and then laughed.

"Do you think I've put it in the best place?" he said, gesturing to the chimney breast. I was worried it might look vain to have a picture of myself on display. I mean, so prominently."

"It's just right," said Lucy. She thought of Rosemary's portrait in the sitting room at Bawson Cottage, hanging conspicuously over the fireplace and reflected in the mirror on the opposite wall. Not that she had seen the picture framed and in position; she wondered, not for the first time, how many people had.

"Of course," Rex added, "what we really need is one of you to go with it. A pendant, so to speak. A pair. Better if it could be by the same artist."

"I don't believe the artist does self-portraits. Anyway, where would a pair live? With you, with me, alternating between the two?"

"That's something we'd have to decide. If the situation arose."

Twenty-two

Lucy and Rex made their way to Bainbridge and Murray together, aiming to arrive about an hour before people were due to be there for the private view. As they turned the final corner, they saw the gallery ahead of them shining in the darkness, the light leeching from the building reflected off the damp pavement. Rex was wearing a fedora – they debated whether it was claret or burgundy but reached no conclusion – and Lucy a matching beret. They had bought them a few days earlier from a stall at Spitalfields market.

They were welcomed by Hebe and Veronica, both wearing name badges for the occasion, but neither had any role this time in dispensing drinks and canapés to the expected crowd. Paul had decided to hire outside caterers, leaving 'the girls', as he called them, free to meet and greet and deal with catalogues and sales.

Paul appeared from his office, wearing his trademark linen suit even in January, and ran through the arrangements for the evening. At the appointed time, he would welcome the assembled company, say a bit about the exhibition, leaving Lucy to say more about her inspiration and approach, and answer any questions. At her insistence, the catalogue itself was devoid of any artist or mission statement. A number of journalists from local, national, and specialist press had been invited, Paul said; the main thing was to ply them with alcohol and otherwise play it by ear.

An hour or so later, Lucy found herself near the gallery's front door where it was cooler and quieter. The opening formalities were over, much to her relief, and she had spent time dutifully circulating and talking to guests. The place was packed and, never good in crowds, she was feeling the panic rise, needed to unwind in calmer space.

"Good turn-out," said Hugh, who had broken away from a group loosely installed in front of some of her metallic paintings. Lucy saw Clare talking to Hugh's wife Kate and waved discreetly. "And a rising tide of red stickers. You must be pleased."

"I know I should be," she said, sounding forlorn. "I'm glad people like the paintings but I'll be sorry to see them go at the end of the show."

"But you've had other shows, sold lots of paintings. It's what you do."

"This seems different somehow, perhaps because it was such an effort. I feel I've invested more of myself in the pictures."

"If it's any consolation," said Hugh, "you'll be able to see one of them in a couple of weeks at Falstaff Road."

"Thank you," said Lucy, smiling bravely.

They were joined by a tall balding man with a small black moustache. Both of them greeted Anthony Buffo, who ran the south London bookshop and gallery where Lucy had had one of her first exhibitions years ago. The exhibition where Barbara Wilcox had bought the picture now hanging in 'the house in Suffolk'! Hugh had been a customer of his for the best part of twenty years.

"Great show," said Anthony. "I'm afraid I've been disloyal," he said, with a suspiciously straight face. "I've been hobnobbing with another artist. A certain Mister Rex Monday. I believe you know him."

"Our paths have crossed," said Lucy. A weak smile had been supplanted by a broad grin.

"As you may know, he met my daughter Caroline in New York last year and mentioned that you had a new series of paintings underway. She meant to pursue the idea of a show with Paul but everything's been up in the air while she moved the gallery from Broome Street to bigger premises round the corner in West Broadway. But she's viewed this exhibition on line and is keen to follow things up."

"I'd love another New York show," she said, becoming animated but sounding wistful. "I'd need enough time to do more work, though. I don't think there's going to be much left after this one. And bigger premises to fill?"

"I may be able to set your mind at rest on that score," said Anthony. "She was thinking of a joint show. Two British artists. Both represented by the same London gallery, as it happens. I gather your paths have crossed."

"Rex! But I wonder what he'd think?"

"It's possible that I mentioned it to him a few moments ago."

"And?"

"I fancy I detected more than a degree of enthusiasm. Though he did say he'd have to talk to Paul about deferring the show he's due to have here."

Lucy went off to find Rex while Anthony talked books with Hugh. A few minutes later, the gallery door opened with a clatter to admit an elderly woman who looked as if she had been blown in by a gust of wind. Unfazed, she put her coat on one of the few remaining hangers and set herself to rights before relieving a passing waiter of a glass of champagne and penetrating the throng.

"You're looking quizzical," said Anthony.

"I think I know that woman," said Hugh, "though I've never met her. The resemblance is uncanny. Long story."

Lucy spotted Rosemary in a corner talking to Barbara Wilcox.

"Good to see you both," said Lucy, uncertain whether to mention Rosemary's interest in the property next door to Barbara's house in Brushwood Road.

"We were saying that you made a handsome couple," said Rosemary, nodding in the direction from which Lucy had come.

"We were," Barbara confirmed. "Rumour has it that his name is Rex. A suitably distinguished name. Regal. I think we should meet him."

She swayed off towards Rex, clearly expecting Rosemary to follow.

"Two things," said Rosemary quickly, "in case I forget to say them later. Lovely to see all your paintings together. Those gothic ones remind me of the summerhouse at home. I'm glad the gallery doesn't charge extra for delivery! Oh, and I've been thinking further about the lodge but I'm sure that can wait."

Lucy was approached by a man with a scribble of ginger hair and a shiny red face. He beamed at her and said,

"Wonderful show, dear, wonderful show." He leaned in and sounded confidential. "I do believe I've detected the influence of Piper with some nods towards Hundertwasser. It's the colour and the shape, the shape and the colour. Am I right or am I right?"

"I admire both, of course," said Lucy, taking a discreet step back. "But I'm not conscious of an influence on my work."

"These things can be unconscious," he said knowingly.

She was rescued by Paul, who said,

"Sorry to interrupt." And then to Lucy, "There's someone you should meet. Two people actually."

They were standing in front of paintings inspired by the stained glass at St Martin's.

"Marion, you know."

She was greeted warmly by Marion Ducasse, owner of the Paris gallery that had shown Lucy's East Anglian paintings. Marion apologised for 'our late arrival', blaming it on delays on the Eurostar.

"And this," said Paul, as if pulling a rabbit out of a hat, "is Jean-Claude Valmy. It's thanks to Marion that he's here."

Jean-Claude bowed and shook her hand.

It took a moment for Lucy to grasp that she was facing the man who had designed the stained glass windows in the church. She took in a man with longish brown curls, designer stubble, and a crumpled blue suit. He looked to be in his mid-thirties. A bit younger than I would have expected, she thought, though she could not immediately say why. He was hardly going to be as old as Matisse when he designed the stained glass in the chapel at Vence.

"I sent Jean-Claude a link to the on-line catalogue," Marion said, "and persuaded him to come with me. Paul tipped me off about the connection. I hope he will forgive me for saying that the catalogue does not do them justice."

Paul muttered something about the limitations of the photographic process in reproducing colour faithfully – "That's why people should come to exhibitions!" – and left them to it.

"Good enough to bring you all this way," said Lucy, feeling embarrassed on Paul's behalf. "Thank you for coming."

"A nice excuse to spend time in London," said Jean-Claude. "And have the pleasure of meeting the artist, of course." His accent, like Marion's, had a slight mid-

Atlantic twang. "You have captured the effects of light passing through glass in a way that I would not have thought possible in pigment. It's as if I only started the process; you have completed it, shown what's it's like to be there, in the church, bathed in coloured light."

Lucy felt herself blushing. She stammered a few words about the brilliance of his coloured glass and the stimulus it had provided for her own work. She asked how he had come to design the stained glass in a church in a small village in Sussex.

"I entered a competition," he said. "They were looking for something non-traditional and happily I won. I only found out about the competition by chance when a colleague saw it advertised and let me know. But what were *you* doing in the church?"

"I was visiting someone nearby and she insisted that I go and see the glass. In fact, she's here this evening; I must introduce you." Lucy did not add that she nearly didn't bother and that, if she hadn't visited the church, Jean-Claude would not be here either. But then how different might things have been if she had not found the notebook, made the connection with number fifty-three, met Rosemary, done her portrait. At best, she thought, it would have been a different show and the poorer for it.

Twenty-three

As the evening drew to a close, Lucy felt both exhilarated and exhausted. Hebe and Veronica were supervising the clearing up while Paul gathered together the small group, Lucy and Rex among them, who were due to make their way to the restaurant he had booked in Shoreditch.

She was glad that she had caught Rosemary again so she could share in person the link between Jean-Claude, St Martin's, and the pictures on the wall. Rosemary was enthusiastic and expansive, making some cryptic comments about the power of art to bring things and people together. People nodded sagely and sipped their champagne.

It turned out that Rosemary was staying with Barbara Wilcox, which was why she had not accepted Lucy's own invitation to stay the night. She had apparently bumped into Barbara when showing her son Clive the lodge site after they had left Lucy that day. They had struck up a friendship of sorts, Lucy learnt to her surprise, Barbara delighted that the place was to be restored rather than redeveloped, 'with who knows what sort of people installed there'.

So Lucy need not have worried, she realised, that the site might prove to be a source of friction between the two women this evening. But when did they discover that they had both met Lucy and had both been invited to the private view?

As Rosemary made for the hangers to retrieve her coat, she said,

"Clive told me I was being too sentimental, hanging on to a building I'd not seen in twenty-five years and which no one left in Brushwood Road had seen at all. No doubt he meant that selling the site for redevelopment would have made a packet. Still, he's back in Australia. You must come and see the lodge properly when it's finished. Rex too. Tell me what you think."

After Rosemary had left with Barbara Wilcox, Rex came up to Lucy.

"That woman," he said. "It's as if the portrait had come to life."

Over the next few days, Paul sent Lucy some early reviews of the show. She was reluctant to look at them until Rex was there.

He scrolled through them slowly, making quiet interjections along the lines of 'Could be worse' or 'Not too awful', without indicating what the reviewer actually thought. Lucy was too nervous to appreciate the teasing.

"Rex! How bad are they?"

"Well...there's this one, headlined *Harmony in Hoxton*:

> *In her new show, Lucy Potter treats us to a dazzling display of chromatic versatility. She eschews the garish for subtle, unusual and effective combinations of colour that complement and do not compete. A magnificent return to form.*

"So speaks Camilla Pemberton in *Art Now!*"

As Lucy said nothing, Rex tried another one.

"How about the redoubtable Glyn Fairlop from *The Art Blog?*

> *Lucy Potter explores the borderland between representation and abstraction in her new series of 'windows' paintings. She does not so much depict as hint at the abundant variety of fenestration, leaving the eye and the imagination of the viewer to complete the process.*

"Or Dan Bluster in *The Hackney Bugle*:

> *Windows! Mundane or what? Who knew there was so much potential in features we are used to looking through rather than at. Welcome to the world of Lucy Potter, who shows us new ways of seeing what's right in front of us. A masterclass in creativity.*

"Perhaps I can interest you in these words from Edna Patullo in *The Review*:

> *It's easy to be seduced by Lucy Potter's use of colour. But these pictures are as much about shape and pattern, texture and the telling detail. For me, it was the gothic windows that won the day. The delicate filagree of tracery evoking lace, the merest suggestion of further windows, conjuring ghosts or shadows.*

"Now, you'll love this one from Fenton Round in *Ace Daubs*:

> *Who said the English don't like colour? Lucy Potter, the Woman Artist from south London with a fondness for fenestration, flings a pot of paint at the magnolia walls of the naysayers and chromophobes.*

Lucy sat up. "*The* Woman Artist *from south London!*" What century are we in? Is he suggesting I should stick to flowers and kittens and children? Let's kidnap Mr Round and dump him in Crystal Palace Park with the other dinosaurs."

"Or we could have a drink," said Rex. "This Man Artist from east London could do with one. I'd say that you – we – have cause for celebration. They obviously liked the exhibition; even Mr Round when you get to the nub of what he's saying."

"I didn't know what to expect," said Lucy. "But the

reviews seem to be all right so far. D'you know Paul said they've sold all the paintings already. Except for a couple of the big ones and even they are reserved for a firm of city solicitors. Quarrendens, the people at Pomona Court who bought some of mine years ago."

"All your months of hard work have paid off. But you're not sounding ecstatic about it."

"I am pleased. Honest. And relieved. It just feels a bit of an anticlimax. And where do I go from here?"

Twenty-four

*I*t was a gloomy day in mid-February and Lucy was having lunch with Clare at Benchers, the wine bar near her chambers at Number One Partridge Court. Clare, having come straight from court, was dressed in funereal black. This did nothing to enliven the proceedings and made the occasion feel rather formal.

They sat at a table well away from the door that let in a blast of cold air whenever it was opened. It was the first time they had enjoyed lunch together for months. They had not spoken at all since the private view, and even then they'd had to make do with a few snatched words as Lucy circulated among the guests.

But they soon relaxed and carried on as if they had spent no time apart. After ordering, they talked a bit about the outcome of the show. Lucy said she had expected a lull afterwards, had been looking forward to it. But there seemed to be no let-up, what with creating new stock for the gallery, commissions for larger pictures for various offices, and beginning to think about the exhibition in New York later in the year. The deadlines were not as demanding but she did not want to let things slip.

"That's a joint one with Rex, isn't it?" said Clare. "New York."

"Yes but he seems to be giving it no thought. I imagine he'll leave everything to the last moment and go into a kind of purdah. I shan't see him."

"How long has it been now, you and Rex?"

"It depends what you take as the starting point. The art school reunion was in June but it was a little while before we got our act together, so to speak."

"And you're still trekking up to Clapton or wherever?"

"Sometimes he comes south of the river. But I usually seem to go to him for some reason."

"Must be a bit wearing," said Clare. "Is that the long-term plan? Maintaining separate places."

"It's what we both need. We have our own space, our own studios."

They paused while the duck and lentils arrived, accompanied by a carafe of the house red.

"Had you thought of getting somewhere together?" said Clare. "At least the living accommodation, possibly renting studio space elsewhere."

"I don't know how that would work," said Lucy. "Who would give up their existing space? I've been at Dogberry Road for twenty years, on and off. I don't want to move and I can't expect him to. Living together apart isn't that unusual, is it?"

"What does Rex think?"

"We haven't discussed it. I don't want to worry him by raising the subject."

"You're not doubting his commitment, I take it?"

"Not at all. Moving would be a big step for both of us."

"I suppose it was different for Paul and me. We sold our own places and bought one together. We didn't need the equivalent of separate studios, though."

They focussed on their food for a while. Then Clare said,

"I bumped into Toby the other day. I haven't seen him for ages. He was asking about the notebook. Specifically, whether you'd had any luck with the rest of it, found out who the girl was, what happened to her. He still seems troubled by what he read."

"What did you say?"

"That her name is Rosemary, you'd located her in Sussex, been to see her, got her life story, painted her portrait."

"I suppose that sums it up," said Lucy, smiling at Clare's ability to cut swiftly through detail and get to the heart of the matter.

"Toby seemed impressed. He asked whether you took commissions. I said the Rosemary portrait was a one-off, especially for her. I hope that was the right answer."

"Yes, apart from the one I did of Rex for Christmas, of course. He keeps pressing me to do a self-portrait. Says his and mine should hang together, though he doesn't say where."

"He's a bit of a romantic on the quiet, isn't he? Why

don't you paint a portrait of yourself anyway and take it from there?"

"Pendants don't have to be by the same artist," said Lucy quietly.

"But surely better if they are, particularly in this case. Isn't that the point? And you'd be in control. Who's going to commission anyone else to do it anyway? Not Rex, I imagine. It seems to me, Miss Potter, that your claim to be an artist who doesn't do people is becoming increasingly hard to sustain!"

Lucy had never liked photographs of herself so the prospect of doing a self-portrait in pastel, as a counterpart to the one she had done of Rex, was both daunting and potentially embarrassing. She had been putting it off, uncertain how to go about it. What would she see, what would others see if the picture ever saw the light of day? And what, who, would it represent?

The idea of staring at herself in a mirror, scrutinising her every feature, dwelling on her imperfections, signs of aging, for hours on end was unappealing and made her feel uncomfortable. But she could not draw an idealised version of herself. It would be dishonest and lack credibility. 'Just be yourself' had been Clare's advice when Lucy confided her anxieties. Easy to say but what did it mean, how would she know whether she was being herself? 'Relax, take it slowly, keep it simple, and draw what you see. You can always have another go if you don't like it.'

Lucy found a mirror, one of those circular double-sided ones on a stand, which she placed on a pile of books on a stool by her easel, removing or adding books as she tried to get the height right relative to where she would be sitting to do the portrait. Her first foray was disconcerting as she had the mirror the wrong way round, hideously exaggerating her features, her eyes enormous, the pores of her skin like lunar craters. She turned the mirror over but quickly realised that it did not show enough of her; she wanted head and shoulders, to match the portrait she had done of Rex. She fetched her grandmother's old dressing table mirror from the chest of drawers in her bedroom and repeated the process of positioning and adjustment.

She wondered what expression to adopt. Would she be able to resist the temptation to laugh? And what about clothes, make-up, jewellery? In the end, she decided to keep things simple, as Clare had suggested, her one concession to adornment being the necklace, of amethyst and silver, that Rex had bought for her in New York. She had a few false starts as she dismissed her first attempts as making her look furtive, shifty, or oddly surprised, like a rabbit caught in the headlights. But she did relax, gradually, and did not notice the time passing as she concentrated on the task in hand. And when, exhausted, she had done as much as she felt she could do she did not know what to think of the result, hating it one moment, conceding that it was not too bad the next. So she turned the easel to the wall and went downstairs to have a drink.

She looked at it again the following day and on

successive days, continuing to blow hot and cold. She kept wondering whether to start again but she had no confidence that the outcome would be materially different. She stared at the portrait, which seemed to be staring back at her, willing her to come to a decision. She took a photograph and sent it, separately, to Rex and to Clare and to Hugh with a simple message: 'Is this me?'

The replies were as simple as the question she had posed. And consistent in their praise, including from Paul to whom Clare had taken the liberty, as she put it, of showing the portrait. Rex was quietly effusive and said he could not wait to see it hanging with 'the other one'.

A few weeks later, Lucy was at the table in her studio staring through the window towards the trees in the distance. It would still be ages, she reflected, before new growth softened their jagged outlines but at least the days were getting longer.

She had just completed a commission for four large windows paintings for the reception area of a merchant bank. The pictures, even unframed, had been so large that Paul had sent a courier to pick them up.

The bank had been surprised when she wanted to see the reception area first. But she needed some idea of context, she'd said, to get a feel of the place, and maybe spot some details, shapes, colours, she might pick up in the pictures themselves. Absurd, in some ways, she told herself. She never knew where people were going to hang her paintings, how they would relate to their new homes. But it was different, she felt, with commissions, when she was producing pictures to go in specific places, even if some corporate clients were looking for little more than a decorative way of filling a space – and perhaps projecting an image as 'patrons of modern art'.

She ought, she knew, to be thinking about work for New York. Her hope that a joint exhibition with Rex would mean that she would have to come up with less herself was proving misplaced. Not having seen the New Romulus Gallery's latest premises, she had not reckoned on its bigger footprint and generous basement. Paul had been discussing what was wanted with Caroline Buffo, owner of the gallery. Her requirements, or expectations, were daunting. And not just for Lucy's work; for Rex's as well. At least if she made a start, she reflected, she'd be in a stronger position to chivvy Rex into making a start too.

Her thoughts were interrupted by the sudden chirrup of her phone. It was a message from Rosemary! Lucy had not heard from her since the private view in January. Rosemary said that progress had been made with refurbishment of the lodge. It was now looking respectable, judging by the photos her project manager had sent her, and ready to receive visitors. Would Lucy and Rex be free to join her to have a look at the place at about noon next Wednesday?

Twenty-five

It was a mild day, lightly overcast, and the pair decided to walk. Lucy had persuaded Rex to tear himself away from his studio the previous evening and spend the night at number thirty-six.

"I'm still not clear what this is about," said Rex. "Or why she wants me there at all."

"I told you. She's following up on what she said at the private view about seeing the lodge when the work was finished. I know something of its history, have heard her talk about it. The place seems to mean a lot to her and I live nearby, of course. What she didn't know, or wasn't saying, when she saw me with her son before Christmas, is what will happen to it. She must have some idea by now, surely."

Rex did not press and they walked the rest of the way in companionable silence. When they arrived at the entrance of the site, Lucy gasped. The hoardings and gates and general detritus had been removed to reveal the lodge that she had never seen, neat, pristine, a miniature house freed from the brambles and the self-sown sycamore. That was the trouble, she thought. What else she had been expecting she could not have said but it had lost the sense of mystery that existed, perhaps, only in her own imagination. And it seemed strangely isolated, out of context, as if it had lost its meaning and purpose in the absence of the house it was built to serve and unrelated to the later houses that now surrounded it. An anomaly, thought Lucy, a delicate Gothic structure in yellow-grey brick quite different in style and scale from its solid Victorian red-brick neighbours.

"It's scrubbed up well," she said feebly.

"It's rather charming," said Rex. "And just like the photograph you showed me of the way it looked years ago. It would lend itself to a pen-and-ink drawing. The building makes a statement in its own small way: I was here first, I am a survivor from an earlier age. It looks a bit stark at the moment but that's because it's newly refurbished. It will tone down and the landscaping you mentioned will soften it further. I'm glad it wasn't knocked down. Odd-shaped site, though. It makes the lodge look wedged in. Like an after-thought, when the opposite is true."

"The site used to be bigger," said Lucy, "but part of the garden was sold to whoever owned number fifty-one at the time." She was rather touched by his first impression of the lodge. She had rarely heard him so voluble. Somehow it mattered that he liked the place even if she felt underwhelmed.

"Are we meeting her inside or outside?" said Rex, looking at his watch.

As Lucy was saying she didn't know, the arrangement hadn't been that specific, a large car hove into view and screeched to a halt at the kerb beside them. It was spattered with mud and looked more like a truck, designed, it seemed, for terrain a good deal more demanding than anything likely to be found in this or any other part of south London. The man at the wheel slipped out. He was wearing a safari jacket and shorts that matched his sandy hair. He greeted them enthusiastically and went round to open the passenger door. Rosemary eased herself onto the pavement and apologised for being late.

"Gary will be back in an hour to pick me up. That should give us plenty of time."

"See you later, Mrs Hartley," said the man, speeding off down Brushwood Road.

"Other clients, other sites," said Rosemary. "Still, he's done a pretty good job here, don't you think? I'm drawing up a planting plan for the grounds, such as they are, though Gary will have to find someone to implement it."

Lucy and Rex were fulsome in their praise, standing back as if assessing the work for the first time. They followed Rosemary up the rough path to the front door, recently stripped and primed. She turned to Lucy and said,

"What colour do you think the door should be painted?" She scrabbled in her bag for the keys. "I was waiting until you'd seen it. I can tell Gary on the way back."

Lucy gulped. "Willow green," she hazarded, looking to Rex for help.

"Sounds good to me," he said. "It'll complement the colour of the brick nicely."

"Thank you," said Rosemary. "It shall be done. Would that all decisions could be made so quickly." She raised the errant keys aloft and proceeded to unlock the door.

It opened directly into what Lucy assumed was, or had been, the sitting room. In the absence of curtains or blinds, the room was unexpectedly bright. Their footsteps echoed on the bare floorboards as they walked around, looking, though there was not much to see.

"I didn't want to change the layout," said Rosemary. "Knock down internal walls, that sort of thing. The kitchen's been redone but I've left the question of carpets and furnishings, here and in the bedroom, until it's clear how the place will be used."

"Have you not decided?" asked Lucy.

"Barbara offered to buy it to use as guest accommodation or a granny annex. Close to number fifty-one but not on top of them, as she put it. There is a certain historical connection, I suppose, so it would make sense from that point of view. But it doesn't feel right, somehow. And, if I sold it to some other buyer, who's to say they wouldn't try to redevelop the site after all? To be honest, I don't need the money. It was never about that, whatever Clive may think. Gordon, for all his other failings, made sure that I've not been short of funds. No," she said firmly. "It's a question of doing what's right, what's appropriate."

Which is what? thought Lucy. You've only said what it isn't.

"So," said Rosemary. "Would this place be any good as a studio?"

"I've got one already," said Lucy. "It's a kind offer, though." She wished she sounded more grateful but she was unprepared, hadn't seen it coming at all.

"I was thinking of Rex." He flushed and seemed about to say something. "You also have a studio, of course," Rosemary continued, "but I believe it's in east London. Not very close to Lucy."

"I don't know what to say," he stammered. "That's very generous. May we have some time to think about it?"

"By all means. I appreciate that it's come out of the blue. Would a week or two suffice? Just to know what you think in principle. There'd be formalities to sort out but it may help if I say that I'm thinking in terms of a peppercorn rent with some sort of safeguard for you when I finally kick the bucket."

Twenty-six

*I*t was September. In less than a month Lucy and Rex would be travelling to New York for their joint exhibition at the New Romulus Gallery. The pictures they were due to show had been completed, framed, packed and despatched, under Paul's supervision, giving the couple a much-needed breathing space before things started again.

They were both exhausted, having combined their work for the exhibition with other commissions and dealing with Rex's move from Clapton and its aftermath. The logistics of moving the contents of his studio to the lodge and the rest of his things to Dogberry Road had not been straightforward and the hiatus had only added to the pressures as deadlines approached.

It was an unsettling time for both of them, a period of adjustment. For while they each retained their separate working space, and spent much of their day alone there uninterrupted, both were losing their private space, their personal domains, places they could call their own. Before the move took place, Lucy had felt apprehensive, excited as she was at the prospect of bringing their lives even closer together. What would it be like to share her house of twenty years, how would it work out, the everyday practicalities? They had spent a lot of time in each other's homes, of course, but had always gone back to their own.

In the weeks following the move, Lucy's qualms evaporated as her home became their home. It felt natural and her fears that number thirty-six would be overwhelmed by Rex and his possessions proved misplaced. He was unsentimental about getting rid of things that duplicated hers and the lodge accommodated much more than she expected. She enjoyed helping him decide where things should go. She found herself looking forward to Rex coming back from his studio each evening, understood if he needed to stay late to finish what he was doing. And he did his share of the cooking!

"I managed to find some yellow courgettes," he said with a small air of triumph one day, "to go with the green ones and the red pepper."

"Traffic lights," said Lucy.

"I could do with some of those black olives, though."

She held the jar aloft and said, with mock strictness,

"I don't give olives to men with inky fingers. I think they need another scrub."

With their pictures safely on their way to New York, Paul was focusing on the art fair in Chelsea, at which he had a stand for the first time in several years.

"I wondered about a rebrand," he said to Lucy when she was in Hoxton one afternoon. "Like BMG or BMG East. A more modern feel, more contemporary. But Clare said that changing it would cause confusion, that we've been known as Bainbridge and Murray for years and people know who we are. I'm not sure I agree – people get used to change more quickly than they think – but perhaps this would not be the best time." Lucy was noncommittal, still attached to the old Cork Street premises where Paul had first shown her work.

He sent Lucy and Rex a complimentary ticket to the fair at the end of the month and they had it with them as they left Sloane Square Station and made their way to the gallery. A heavy rain shower ended as abruptly as it had started and a dull pewter sky became a stately Wedgwood blue in no time at all. Brilliant sunshine dazzled on wet pavements. Lucy took Rex's arm and they sidestepped puddles together. Through the archway, avoiding dripping plane trees, they approached the massive portico of the gallery building. Once inside, they studied the floor plan and looked for the Bainbridge and Murray stand.

"Gallery 9 on the first floor," said Lucy, tapping the plan. "It's in the corner."

They were in no hurry and were content to wander, to get their bearings. Lucy was struck by the variety and quality of work on offer and by the distinctive personalities of the individual stands, some minimalist, some cluttered, many enhanced by items of antique furniture for the display of catalogues, sculpture and other small items. Dealers paced, fondled their lanyards, took close interest in their mobile phones, greeted friends and old clients with extravagant gestures. Sales were made, address books signed, contact details left for future reference.

Lucy found herself staring at some drawings of cats by Gwen John. They were in the company of Henry Moore sheep and a flower painting by Winifred Nicholson.

"That one looks just like Ozymandias when he sits on one of my garden chairs," she said. "A bit out of my league, though," she added, nodding at the price. "You know, going round the fair brings home the value of what Rosemary has at Bawson Cottage. And that's just in the sitting room. I wonder if she has any idea."

"I doubt she'd care," said Rex. "They're part of a home of many years, part of her surroundings. Part of her, you could say. Not that I've seen them, of course."

As they were coming away, Rex lowered his voice and said, "The man at that stand has a suit so sharp I'm surprised he hasn't cut himself. Is there a first aid post?"

They came upon Paul sitting at his corner stand on the first floor, the words 'Bainbridge and Murray' high on each wall in bold black letters. Odd, thought Lucy, to see him out of context, one dealer among many rather than lord of all he surveyed. In this setting, he looked less confident than usual, a little tentative, cutting a rather isolated figure perched on his tubular chair.

"How's it going?" she asked as Paul rose to greet them.

"Not bad," he said, gesturing to several wrapped canvases leaning against the wall behind his chair and awaiting collection.

"I see no gaps," said Rex.

"I have a cupboard," said Paul. He pulled open a section of wall to reveal rows of pictures neatly arranged on their sides. "Reserve stock. One painting sells, another takes its place. The trick is to have a variety, something of everything in the hope you'll hit the mark."

Lucy spotted two of her own paintings, a safe distance from a piece of Terry Truant's street art. A late abstract and one of her East Anglian series.

"No Potters sold yet, I'm afraid," said Paul, following her gaze, "but it's early days."

"Of course," said Lucy, producing a smile, not sure whether she minded or not.

"One of Rex's prints went from the browser, though."

An elderly couple drifted onto the stand and showed interest in the work on display. Lucy said they'd be back later and they left Paul to it. Hebe, she gathered, was due to join him later; she was glad that he would be having some company, some support.

Lucy and Rex continued their tour in the company of David Hockney, Bridget Riley, Howard Hodgkin and many other artists well known or less well known. After a while, Lucy said, "I think I've seen enough pictures of lemons in blue bowls to keep me going. Let's go and have some coffee."

Rex said he'd join her in a few minutes. She went up to the second floor and found the café. It was hot and heaving and it took her a while to get served and find anywhere to sit. By the time Rex arrived – 'a few minutes' was more than twenty – the coffee was lukewarm but he seemed so excited, bursting to say something, that she didn't have the heart to complain.

"Guess what I've seen," he said.

"I sense you're going to tell me."

"A painting – a portrait – by none other than Charles House."

"Not *our* Charles House?" said Lucy, sitting up. She hadn't heard that name in years. He had taught them both at art school and had encouraged Lucy to take up portrait painting, praised her early efforts, set her on a course that she abandoned when she found that her work – one portrait in particular – was not appreciated. She had avoided 'doing people' ever since, until that day at Bawson Cottage.

"The very same; the style is unmistakable."

"I wonder what it's doing here. I mean, I didn't know his work had a market. I've never seen his pictures come up."

"Good that he's valued," said Rex. "Shows it's never too late."

Soon afterwards, they were at the stand of Chanticleer

Fine Art, looking at the picture by Charles House. A portrait in oils of a girl, young woman, with long brown hair. Just head and shoulders, freely done.

"Reminds me a bit of you when you were at art school," said Rex.

Lucy flushed. "It doesn't say who it is," she said quickly. "I don't suppose we'll ever know. Don't they say that all portraits are ultimately self-portraits, regardless of the subject. As you say, his style is unmistakable."

"According to the label he's still alive; at least, it only gives a date of birth."

They were approached by Chanticleer's proprietor, Nigel Gosling, a man with a brick-red face that matched his trousers.

"Still alive," he said, "but not too well, I fear, and perhaps not long for this world. The picture came from his studio, along with a number of others. The family seem anxious to make some progress in clearing the place. The portrait, as you see, is undated but my guess is that House painted it about thirty years ago when he was still teaching. He obviously hung on to it."

Yes, he did, thought Lucy. Perhaps no one wanted to buy it at the time. They thanked him for the information and he moved away to speak to other potential customers.

"It would be nice to have something by Charles House and it's not a bad price," said Rex. "What do you think?"

Lucy was quiet for a moment and then said, "We already know his work. This is a chance for others to find him, for him to be better known, to get some sort of recognition. I'd like that."

They turned to leave the stand, Rex pausing to take a photo of the portrait. He picked up one of Chanticleer's cards from a glass-topped table, slipped it into his pocket and made his way with Lucy to the next gallery.

They were talking about calling in again on Paul, when they came to an abrupt halt at the stand of Tipping and Chance.

"Look," squealed Lucy. "It's one of mine! One of the windows pictures I sold at the Christmas show last year."

They moved closer to the picture, which was flanked by a Paula Rego and a Barbara Hepworth.

"Bloody hell," said Lucy, looking at the price. "It's more than trebled in nine months. Do you suppose Paul has seen it?"

Rex approached Orlando Tipping, a tall thin man with an emerald green bow tie and floppy hair the colour of wet sand.

"I was wondering what you could tell me about that painting of a gothic window. And about the artist. Lucy...*Potter*, did it say on the label?"

"Ah yes," said Mr Tipping, pushing his horn-rimmed glasses up the bridge of his nose. "Wonderful colours, don't you think. It's a recent work, one of a series, by an established artist. She's versatile too; you never know what she'll do next."

"Prolific?"

"In phases, I believe. But the paintings rarely appear in the secondary market."

"People must want to keep hold of them," said Rex. "Though not this one, apparently." He peered at the label. "Provenance: a private collector."

"More than that I cannot say."

"Quite so. A good investment?"

"I'd never advise buying solely for investment. It tends to be a long-term game and an uncertain one. Buying what you like is the safest way and the most satisfying."

"Thank you for your time. What's the best way of getting hold of you if I'd like to take things further?"

Mr Tipping produced two cards and gave them to Rex. "This is me; the other one is Annabel Chance. Either of us would be happy to help."

They managed to get to the lifts before Lucy burst out laughing. And then she said,

"Do you think I'm a good investment?"

"I certainly do," said Rex. "Your paintings aren't bad either."

"Idiot," she said, giving him a hug. "Let's find Paul."

It was still sunny when Lucy and Rex left the fair. They walked slowly down the King's Road, taking in sights and sounds. Knots and drifts of tourists strewn across the pavement; a one-man steel band installed between lamp post and bollard; many red buses moving sedately, as if in convoy; a disconcerting display of mannikins, headless and armless, in a dress shop window. Lucy was struck by the blandness of much of the clothing in the windows they passed, a pair of purple ankle boots ("'Heliotrope', if you please, Miss Potter: look at the label."), offering a welcome relief. She was tempted, but not very.

They continued past entrances to fashionable squares until they found a café that looked fairly quiet. Sitting at the back with sandwiches and more coffee, they reflected on their conversation with Paul.

"He didn't seem too worried, or surprised, by the price Tipping and Chance were asking for my picture," said Lucy.

"It'll be interesting to see if they get it," said Rex.

"That's what Paul said." She suddenly stopped, sandwich in mid-air. "I hope he didn't think I was complaining that he was selling my stuff too cheap. I'd be mortified. I didn't mean that at all."

"I know you didn't and I'm sure he does too. Don't worry about it."

They were both silent for a while. Rex stared at his empty cup, toyed with packets of sugar, shifted in his chair. Lucy sensed that he was about to say something. And then he did,

"You've come so far in the last year or so. You were in a bit of a bad way when we met after the reunion."

"I felt wretched," said Lucy. "I didn't think I'd be able to paint again. And without painting I knew I couldn't be me. Not properly. I was slow to get my confidence back and believe in myself as I developed the windows pictures and gradually overcame the block."

"Not to mention the portraits," said Rex. "With *me*, it's more of the same and even that's a struggle. But with you… What was it Orlando Tipping said? 'She's versatile too; you never know what she'll do next.' And in pretty good company between Paula Rego and Barbara Hepworth."

"Thank you," said Lucy quietly. "I couldn't have done it without you. Your support means a lot to me. As do you. And all that business with Rosemary and her portrait has helped me see things differently, look at people differently. Inspiration can come from unexpected places. But it's windows and only windows for the time being."

Twenty-seven

*L*ucy was excited to be back in New York. It was not just the prospect of the show and of seeing Caroline Buffo again but the vibrancy and vitality of the city itself. There was nothing like it to energise, to lift the spirits. And this time Rex was with her.

They arrived the weekend before their exhibition was due to open at the New Romulus Gallery. It was an afternoon in mid-October, still pleasantly warm but much cooler, Rex said, than it had been during his visit to the city in the summer of the year before. They were heading on the subway for a hotel in Tribeca, conveniently located about ten minutes' walk from the gallery. It had been recommended by Stephen Marling, whom Lucy knew from her brief stay in his south London square some years ago while another artist borrowed her Norfolk cottage. Stephen divided his time between London and New York and they were due to meet him, and his partner Nancy Steiner, for a meal that evening. Lucy hoped she could stay awake.

The days leading up to their departure had been

hectic. Paul had suddenly decided, after the fair, that there was some publicity mileage in two London artists, a couple no less, about to fly off to hold a joint exhibition in a New York gallery. A double manifestation of a special relationship, he said, and warned them that Caroline Buffo was thinking on similar lines. She was whipping up interest and having some success. Their stay in New York was unlikely to be quiet!

Paul's first thought was to 'have the journos' up to Bainbridge and Murray in Hoxton. But it then occurred to him that Rex's studio at the lodge offered a much more attractive backdrop for interviews and photographs than a utilitarian structure in east London. And a quaint small building with gothic windows would add a useful romantic element and resonate nicely with Lucy's paintings.

Paul was not wrong. Pictures of Lucy and Rex standing in the landscaped front garden, with the lodge behind, appeared on-line and on-screen. Barbara Wilcox sent Rosemary a link to the piece featuring on BBC London news; Rosemary was reported to be 'tickled pink'. He was right too about the portraits, the one Lucy had done of Rex and the one she had done of herself as a companion piece. The two pictures had hung together at Dogberry Road before being lent to the New Romulus Gallery to accompany the New York show. Paul had released images of the portraits to the press with the other publicity material, both as a counterpart to the official photographs of the artists and, he admitted later, as a showcase for Lucy's wider talents and a possible future direction. The portraits attracted praise but not to the extent of overshadowing the current work, which was widely admired.

Paul – Lucy and Rex agreed – was a slick operator. "Paul and Clare both," said Rex. "They deserve each other." It had emerged some while after he had consented to move south that it was Clare who had suggested to Rosemary that she offer the lodge to Rex as a studio as a way of bringing him and Lucy closer together, geographically and perhaps more. Clare had apparently got Rosemary's number from Hugh, saying that some sort of nudge was needed.

"Hugh called me a *dea ex machina*," Clare said to Lucy over the phone one evening. It was, they agreed, the kind of thing he said.

Lucy and Rex were meeting Stephen and Nancy at eight o'clock, which was one o'clock in the morning London time. They were beginning to flag. Their route to the restaurant took them past the gallery on the other side of West Broadway. They stopped and stared across the traffic, barely conscious of the rush and roar of it. The gallery was much more impressive, they decided, than the previous premises round the corner in Broome Street. It was an imposing building, painted slate grey, with steps up to the front door flanked by fluted columns topped by capitals of no known classical order. At the bottom of the steps, on either side, stone urns planted with ferns and ivy added a note of freshness and sophistication. Rex pointed to the date – 1872 –

picked out in gold in the pediment above the building's façade and gently illuminated by an unseen light. Lucy wondered what the building had been used for then and what it was before the gallery moved in.

They crossed the road to have a better look. The urns, Lucy noticed, were discreetly chained to the steps. A small sign to one side of the door projected from the building at right angles. It swung in the gentle breeze and bore the letters: NRG. No more and no less. Perhaps, she thought, Paul had a point about rebranding Bainbridge and Murray as BMG!

In the window, a large poster announced the forthcoming exhibition of work by two British artists, Rex Monday and Lucy Potter. "Purely alphabetical order of surname," said Rex, who seemed embarrassed that his name came first. Lucy was not concerned, focussing on the details of each of their works shown on the poster and on the pastel portraits of the two artists, reproduced in miniature.

"It's official," she said. "We're here!"

She turned away, suddenly feeling giddy, light-headed. She blamed the effects of the journey and the length of time they had been up. She took Rex's arm and they made their way to the restaurant, an Italian place near Canal Street.

They woke early the next day and spent time wandering streets near the Hudson while they waited for a local diner to open. Despite last night's meal, Rex had no difficulty in demolishing a stack of blueberry pancakes with a side order of bacon while Lucy had a more modest, but nevertheless substantial, bowl of yoghurt, granola and fresh fruit. So they took a roundabout route to the gallery, involving several detours, mostly intentional, as they walked off their breakfast and explored areas they did not know.

Caroline and Lucy greeted each other effusively, each claiming that the other 'hadn't changed a bit' in the years since they had seen each other. In fact, Caroline's glossy black hair was shorter than Lucy remembered, more stylish, and the quantity of jewellery surely increased, the gold rings on her fingers flashing in the light of the gallery spots.

Lucy and Rex complimented her on the new premises as she gave them a preview of the exhibition opening the following week. "No white walls!" said Lucy ecstatically. The layout lent itself to different colours on different walls: dove grey and indigo (Lucy), pale terracotta and sage green (Rex). Each had pictures on both floors and the main displays of their work were accompanied by the originals of their portraits. They had seen the catalogue on-line but it gave no hint of how the pictures would appear in the gallery itself.

"It makes me look like a proper artist," said Lucy.

"You and me both!" said Rex.

This was, she realised, the first time she had seen Rex's pictures displayed in this way. Glimpses of work in progress or prints in a browser at Bainbridge and Murray were one thing, a small selection hanging cheek by jowl with many others at the Christmas show another. But here, brought together and prominent on the walls, were examples of the range of his work – engravings, woodcuts, drawings in pen and ink – detailed and delicate and presenting a marked contrast to her own. As if Lucy had voiced her thoughts, Caroline came up to her and said,

"Two completely different approaches but working well together and reinforcing, enhancing, each other. But what they have in common is a certain quintessential Englishness, as one or two people have pointed out to me. Not so easy for us to notice but I see it as a selling point in these parts!"

Caroline confirmed that she had been drumming up media interest in the exhibition and that the private view was 'likely to be heaving'. Lucy kept quiet about her difficulties with crowded places, tried to sound pleased that so many people were due to attend. Caroline became excited when Lucy said that Stephen Marling and Nancy Steiner would be coming. She immediately focussed on the publicity value: for Nancy, after years of getting nowhere in her acting career, had at last had a break and was currently filming the second series of a show on Netflix. Her name and face were recognised. This no doubt explained, Lucy reflected, the knowing looks from customers and staff at the restaurant last night. None of which had inhibited Nancy from crooning 'Two Englishmen in New York', perhaps a little too loudly, with reference to Stephen and Rex. They'd looked amused and embarrassed in equal measure as people at nearby tables burst into applause.

Caroline was even more impressed when Rex added that Nancy said she would mention the exhibition on social media and try to persuade various acting friends to come or at least spread the word. And then Lucy revealed that she and Rex had been invited to a party at Nancy's next week and that the invitation extended to Caroline too. It was in the nature of a belated flat-warming, said Lucy, as Nancy had been able to give up her room at the top of a Park Slope brownstone and buy an apartment nearby. She had also given up her job at Prospect Books, a regular haunt of Caroline's father, Anthony Buffo, when he was visiting New York.

Conversation turned to logistical matters and the handling of media activity. As Lucy and Rex were about to set off to some lunchtime jazz in Greenwich Village, Caroline said,

"Hang on; I nearly forgot the books."

She lifted the cloth on a table near the door and pulled out two boxes. She put them on the table and carefully removed the contents. They were all American editions of books illustrated by Rex. Caroline produced a pen and asked Rex to sign the title page of each copy. When he had finished, she said,

"I was thinking of having this one open on the table. It's rather charming, don't you think?"

She held a page illustrated with a woodcut, in black and white, of two doves on the branch of a tree.

"Good choice," said Lucy, smiling hugely. Rex did not demur.

Caroline put the book back on the table and opened the door.

"Mind the pumpkins on the stoop," she said. "You can't move for them in New York at this time of year."

Lucy and Rex went carefully down the steps, turned and waved, before heading to Greenwich Village.

Twenty-eight

Lucy was sitting at the table in her studio staring out of the window. The sky this dank November morning was uniformly grey and featureless. She felt as gloomy as the day itself after the warmth and energy of New York. Even the fiery red leaves of the acer that had cheered them on their return now lay sodden on the grass below and the branches of the fig were bare for another year.

The last year had been both exhausting and exhilarating. The Christmas show at Bainbridge and Murray, her own exhibition at the gallery, the joint one with Rex in New York. Successes all but now they were over she felt deflated and disillusioned. She knew she needed the rest, ought to welcome the opportunity to recharge her batteries. Yet with nothing further on the horizon, nothing specific to aim for, she had difficulty stirring herself, making herself think about the few commissions that she was supposed to be tackling. What would she do this time if the block came back?

The sudden crack of an unseen firework in a

neighbour's garden brought her to with a jolt. And then sight of Rex, emerging from the shed, rake in hand. He should be in his studio at the lodge. Rex at least had the prospect of his own show in Hoxton but he too found it hard to focus, shared her sense of anticlimax now they were back.

★

The New Romulus Gallery had been packed on opening night. Lucy and Rex were much in demand, both separately and as a couple, and that helped her cope with crowd and crush. The interest was reflected in sales of both their works and the pile of Rex's signed books quickly shrank and disappeared. Caroline retreated to the relative calm of her office to message the publishers for extra supplies.

"Did you know I had a British accent?" said Lucy, passing Rex on the stairs. "I've been told several times already."

The late arrival of Nancy Steiner, accompanied by Stephen Marling and a trio of her Netflix co-stars, caused a further flurry of interest and gave Lucy and Rex a brief respite as phones were lifted from pocket and bag and photos posted on social media. And then the artists themselves, all shiny foreheads and silly grins, were summoned to take their places for photographs with the visitors.

"Great publicity!" said Caroline. "Maybe I should get a red carpet."

But it was an even later arrival that caught Lucy

by surprise. A grey-haired man, tall and tanned, was hovering by the door, having just, it seemed, come through it. He was looking around, perhaps for a drink, perhaps for anyone he knew. Clive Hartley!

"What on earth are you doing here?" said Lucy, as she wove towards him. "Delighted to see you."

She lifted a glass of champagne from a silver salver and passed it to him, then steered to a space by the book table. It was about the only place in the gallery, she said, they'd be able to hear themselves think.

"I'm gatecrashing," Clive said. "I'm in New York on business and heard about the show by chance earlier today. I thought I'd come along and say 'Hi'."

Another chance meeting, thought Lucy, recalling his unexpected appearance with Rosemary at her own front door. He was more relaxed without his mother but no less softly spoken, which made it difficult, even in the spot that Lucy had chosen, to sustain conversation above the hubbub.

"You must meet Rex," she said, turning to see if he was nearby. The throng seemed impenetrable.

"Love to, but this doesn't look like the ideal moment. Would you and Rex be free for a meal at the Tribeca Grill tomorrow night? Say, eight o'clock? I'll try and slip out at lunchtime to come and have a proper look at the show. Congratulations, by the way. Great turnout."

Lucy accepted the invitation with alacrity, hoping that neither Rex nor Caroline nor anyone else had other plans. Clive downed his champagne and left to go down the steps to West Broadway. She realised, too late, that she had no way of getting in touch with him if there was a problem.

In the event, there was no problem. Lucy worried that Rex would feel the evening had been hijacked but he said he was intrigued to meet Clive. What would a son of Rosemary be like? And what was it like being her son?

They met him at the appointed time and place, only a few minutes' walk from their hotel. Chatting in a preliminary sort of way as they settled at their table, it turned out that their paths had almost crossed at NRG earlier that day. Rex had called in to sign the extra copies of books couriered to the gallery after selling out last night. He left with Lucy shortly before Clive arrived to view the exhibition.

"Great show," said Clive. "Two completely different styles that work well together. Complement each other, you might say. I picked up a copy of the catalogue. It doesn't do the pictures justice, of course, but it gives a good overview. I treated myself to one of the paintings inspired by the stained glass at St Martin's. I know the church; the new glass was installed shortly before I left for Australia. My mother wanted me to see it. The sun obliged by coming out while we were there. You've captured the moment."

"Thank you," said Lucy, who could see that he was moved.

"Don't know when I'll get the picture. It'll be shipped to me in Sydney after the show's over. But there's one picture I can take back with me."

He bent down and opened his case. With a flourish, he produced one of Rex's prints. It was a reproduction of his pen-and-ink drawing of the lodge. Rex had given the original to Rosemary to thank her for letting him use it as a studio.

"My turn to say thank you," said Rex.

"My mother," said Clive, "sent me a photo of the drawing you gave her so I knew of it already. Not that I've ever seen the building itself; the site had a hoarding around it when the place was being refurbished and I never went there in the old days. But that doesn't mean it's not important to me. The lodge is part of the family history, going back to the time it really was the lodge to the big house which my ancestors owned. My mother seemed to think I'd want to knock it down and redevelop the site. I'd never have done that. But perhaps she was making a point by sending me the photo, to show me how things had turned out, what would have been lost. Either way, she made the right decision to restore it and it's being put to the right use."

A waiter was lurking to take their orders. They had not even looked at the menus. Clive quickly scanned the wine list and chose a bottle of Sancerre 'to tide us over', as he put it. He slipped the picture back in his case while they decided what to eat.

During the course of the evening, prompted by gentle questioning from both Lucy and Rex, they gleaned a little of life at Bawson Cottage in the 1970s and 1980s.

"Much of the time I wasn't there, of course, being

away at school and then university. Which made me appreciate it all the more when I was. Stability and continuity, I suppose. A place you know you can come back to, where nothing much changes, isolated and insulated from the wider world. Life and work have taken me away but I'd like to move back in the next few years. Don't know how the family would take to that."

"To Bawson Cottage?" asked Lucy, as she tackled her baby beets.

"Yes. When the time comes, as they say, if not before. Robust as my mother appears, I could see that she was beginning to struggle when I was in England last year. Not that she'd admit it but maybe the portrait she asked you to do was her way of outlasting herself, if you see what I mean. A token of farewell. Still being around when she's no longer around."

"You didn't have a dull childhood, I'm guessing," said Rex. "When you were at home."

"My father wasn't much in evidence during the week. I spent time with my mother, mostly, when I wasn't exploring the beech woods. We went all over the place, sometimes to the coast or downs, sometimes visiting people I didn't know she knew. She was keen that I played with other children, made friends, at least in the holidays. She said she'd not forgotten what it was like to be an only child. Other than that, my mother never talked about her childhood. I didn't even know she'd done those flower paintings yet she must have kept them with her for seventy years or more."

Clive paused, then added,

"In retrospect, she seemed anxious to be a good mother, almost trying too hard."

"And your father?" asked Rex.

"Hearty. Matey. Not much given to displays of affection. Preferred rituals like kicking a football round the garden with me. Because he thought that was the sort of thing fathers did. The atmosphere at home seemed to change when he was around. I'm not sure why. Things between my parents were cordial enough, as far as I could tell, but perhaps a little lacking in warmth. Hard to put my finger on it."

Clive topped up everyone's glasses and turned his attention to the tuna tartare he had hardly touched. Lucy let him make progress. It sounded as though he knew nothing of what his mother had endured as daughter or wife. Perhaps Rosemary found it easier to 'spill the beans' to a virtual stranger, lacking the family baggage. But there was another question Lucy wanted to ask before the branzino arrived, feeling that a new course would change the dynamics and the direction of conversation.

Finally, she said,

"I was sorry to hear that your father died…in an accident, wasn't it?"

"That's right," said Clive, spearing the last piece of avocado on his plate. "Long time ago now. He fell into the river, was swept away and drowned. My mother saw it happen. Nothing she could do, she said. I was living in London by then. The funeral was at St Martin's, with flowers from the garden. Things they had grown together. Rather a nice touch, when you think about it."

Clive ordered another bottle and they talked about his own family in Australia and what they did. When the time came to go, Clive insisting on paying, he said they must get together again when he came to England next year.

"Just a visit, not the move. But I warn you, I may bring my whole mob with me!"

They liked Clive, they decided, as they made their way back to the hotel and an early night. A busy day ahead, with interviews arranged for morning and afternoon and Nancy Steiner's flat-warming in Brooklyn in the evening.

"I think we can trust him to value Rosemary's things, look after them," said Lucy. "I was worried that her possessions, her life, would be dismantled and dispersed without a thought."

"*We?*" said Rex. "Do we have a locus in this matter, Miss Potter?"

"You sound like Clare. I wonder what he'll find, though, 'when the time comes', what else she's squirrelled away? Let's hope there are a few years yet."

★

"Very therapeutic," said Rex when he came in from raking up leaves. "I suppose I ought to go to the studio and confront a blank page."

"I need to do something," said Lucy. "Get out of the house."

"Walk in the woods?"

"Something different."

By the time Lucy and Rex reached Battersea Park, the sun was shining fitfully in a pale blue sky between puffs of cloud, grey and white. They had coffee sitting beside the lake, unbothered by the diving and screeching of gulls, as they followed the stately progress of a pair of swans and the antics of moorhens chasing across the water. The day was becoming unseasonably warm and they reluctantly decided it was time to move. They ambled towards the river, barely aware of the joggers and cyclists streaming past, tennis players thrashing on the courts close by, frantic activity that, on another day, might have left Lucy feeling indolent, the victim of a largely sedentary life.

They passed under plane trees, the rough bark pleasingly gnarled and knobbly. By the time they neared their goal, she was almost cheerful. And then, at sight of the parapet wall along the river, remembrance of Gordon Hartley's fate flashed back. For a split second she felt, illogically, that a similar fate was about to befall her, that she would be swept helpless downstream. The moment passed but she remained tense, fearful. She stood for a while, holding the guard rail, Rex beside her, staring at the water sparkling in the sun, the gentle bobbing of boats at their moorings. Restful, calming. And barges loaded with sand heading upstream, evidence of a working river, a sense of continuity, that she found reassuring.

They sat down on a bench near the pagoda. A hairy man with a hairy dog approached, then veered off towards Albert Bridge.

"Is it dogs who grow to look like their owners," said Rex, "or the other way round?"

The sudden chirrup of Lucy's phone was matched by the buzz of Rex's. "A duet!" said Rex, but their faces fell as they read the message both had received as members of the art school group established after the reunion last summer. Charles House, they learnt, had died the previous day.

"Oh no," said Lucy. The death of her former tutor, he'd taught them both, yet another reminder of mortality, the temporary nature of things. His age the same as her parents. And ten years younger than Rosemary. "Funeral TBA. We ought to go."

"That dealer at the art fair, Nigel Gosling, said Charles wasn't well. It was less than two months ago."

"I wonder how he got on with selling pictures from Charles's studio? What was the name of the firm?"

"Chanticleer Fine Art," said Rex.

Lucy had a look at the website. There were six pictures by Charles House, of which two had apparently been sold. A still life (*Chrysanthemums in a green jug*) and the portrait of a young woman with long brown hair they'd seen at the fair. She stared at the portrait for some moments, enlarging it and restoring it before passing her phone to Rex.

"At least it's a start," she sighed, "in his work getting wider attention."

★

"It is you, isn't it?" said Rex.

They were on their way back from the crematorium, having decided not to attend the wake afterwards in a hotel some miles away. The chapel had been packed for the funeral. Just inside the entrance, displayed on an easel, a portrait of the artist as a young man, a self-portrait of Charles House in yellow flared trousers and an Afghan coat. Early 1970s, by the look of it, thought Lucy, as she stood in front of the painting, remembering the man who had painted that picture of her almost a quarter of a century later. She wasn't sure why she had been reluctant to confirm it at the fair or when looking at the gallery's website as they sat in the park. There were no bad memories. She had been happy to sit for the artist when he asked her and was touched that he had kept it. Or perhaps it really was that no one had wanted to buy it. Now, the portrait just seemed irrelevant, a relic of another time, a snapshot of a person she no longer was.

"Yes," she said. "As I was thirty years ago. Like a fly caught in amber. A curiosity. Not the person I am now."

"You could say that of any photograph taken at a particular moment in someone's life. It doesn't mean trying to preserve them in aspic or preferring them as they were. It's just a record."

"A spirited defence, Mr Monday."

"Well, that picture means a lot to me, as a reminder of the person I first met all those years ago. No comparison with the current version, of course."

"You don't mean that you…"

Rex nodded. He looked sheepish, but not very.

How could she be cross with him? "I was beginning to wonder when I saw Nigel Gosling greet you like a long lost friend in the garden of remembrance. Where is it?"

"She's swathed in bubble wrap in my studio. In what used to be the bedroom."

"You'd better unwrap her before she suffocates," said Lucy. "And put her on a wall."

Lucy had finished her remaining commissions – four large windows pictures, all collages, destined for the conference room of a firm in Belgravia. Paul had sent a courier to pick them up and she was left with an empty space in her studio.

When Rex came back from his own studio that evening, he said,

"I had a strange encounter this afternoon. The boy from number fifty-one knocked on the door of the lodge and asked me if I was a spy. I told him I was but that I was working undercover as an artist. He agreed to keep it secret and ran off satisfied."

"Henry Wilcox!" said Lucy. "Don't encourage him. Well, *I've* spent the day thinking about bricks."

"Why?"

"A future direction, maybe; something to explore."

"Too late! They were done by Carl Andre years ago."

"Not actual bricks. Pictures of brick*work*. Buildings, railway arches, and so on. Think of the colours: yellow, black, grey, plum, pink, red… And the relationship with other materials: wood, tile, slate, stucco, render, metal, glass… The shapes and textures, different lighting conditions. Some close up, some further away."

"Sounds really interesting," said Rex, "with a lot of possibilities. But you said you would only be doing windows for the time being. You're not abandoning them, are you? They've been such a success, brought you a whole new audience."

"No. I need to look ahead, though. I can't keep doing the same thing indefinitely."

"They're not all the same. That's the point. They're all different."

"But variations on a theme," said Lucy. "I shan't do anything hasty or turn down work in the meantime."

After supper that evening, Lucy's phone rang. It was Paul.

"Sorry to ring you at this hour but I'd thought you'd like to know. I've had a call from Marion Ducasse. Seems that Jean-Claude Valmy was much taken with your stained glass pictures at the private view. The ones of St Martin's that he designed."

Lucy had not forgotten what Jean-Claude had said. It was almost a year ago! *'You have captured the effects of light passing through glass in a way that I would not have thought possible in pigment.'*

"He and Marion want you to do a whole series inspired by his stained glass in other churches and chapels in France."

"I've seen them on his website," said Lucy. "They look even more spectacular."

"This would involve going to visit them, to get a sense of the effects of colour and light *in situ*. With a view to an exhibition at Marion's gallery in Paris. It would be a great opportunity to take your windows pictures a step further."

"When would this be?"

"There are a lot of details to sort out but sometime next year. Preferably when there's a decent chance of some sun. By the way, the portraits of you and Rex are back from New York at last. I'll have them brought round in the morning."

Lucy was keen to put the portraits back on the wall before Rex came home from the studio. She removed two watercolours by Rosemary – apple blossom and Japanese quince – that had been keeping the space above the fireplace and hung the portraits in the gaps. Back in their rightful places, side by side: Rex to the left, Lucy to the right. Both looked relaxed, with approving smiles she had not noticed before, as if there was nowhere else they would rather be.

Also by Christopher Bowden

The Blue Book

Fear death by water. D.

The discovery of a cryptic note hidden inside a second-hand book sends thirty-something Hugh Mullion on an obsessive search for its previous owner. Hugh uncovers secrets that have lain hidden for sixty years and turn upside down his views of personal identity and the certainty of the past. Along the way, Hugh learns more about himself and what he really wants from his relationship with his partner, Kate – and about the puzzling disappearances of Anthony Buffo, in whose shop Hugh found the book that changed everything.

"…an intriguing and affecting story written with élan… the kind of book that readers love."

The Yellow Room

When Jessica Tate finds an old country house guide in a box after her grandmother's funeral she is drawn into a mystery that has remained unsolved for over half a century and is set to change her life forever. Intrigued by the house and the family that lived there, she is propelled into a world of disappearances and deceptions, eventually unlocking the secret of the Yellow Room itself.

As the shadows lift, a picture emerges of a landed family fighting to stem the decline in its fortunes in a post-war world in which Britain's own role is steadily declining.

"…a rare glimpse into our recent history, far too rarely plundered by modern novelists, and deftly done." *Andrew Marr*

"A novel as intriguing as the house at its heart. I loved it." *Julian Fellowes*

"…quintessentially English…an intriguing book, full of family mysteries and deception." *Oxford Times*

The Red House

Her face was thinner than it used to be, tauter somehow, almost gaunt, and the eyes seemed troubled. The hair, once long and flowing, was cut roughly short. Almost hacked, he thought. Yet it was surely her...

When Colin Mallory sees a sketch of a young actress he once knew on display in the local market, memories of their past together are brought back sharply to the surface. Alarmed by her distressed appearance, Colin is propelled on a search that draws him into the nightmare world of 'the group' and the sinister influence that threatens to control him too.

This is an engrossing story of artifice and hidden secrets, rich with theatrical detail and a cast of compelling characters.

"Very entertaining, cleverly constructed and expertly paced. I thoroughly enjoyed it." *Sir Derek Jacobi*

The Green Door

BEATRICE NEWTON
1876 – 1887
She fell asleep too soon

Clare Mallory has a Victorian mourning locket with the photograph of a girl and a curl of her hair. When Clare loses the locket in a fortune-teller's tent her quest to find it draws her into a dark episode of the family's past and the true circumstances of the girl's untimely death at Danby Hall, her Norfolk home.

The locket has been taken by the fortune-teller herself, sensing a troubled history and danger ahead. But her attempts to understand the warning signs release forces long held at bay. Events of the past seep into the present until the reappearance of a man who vanished from Danby Hall in 1887 threatens not only her life but Clare's too.

"Draws the reader in immediately and has all the elements of an intriguing mystery. In short, a page-turner. The heroine, Clare, is engaging and Madame Pavonia a suitably exotic yet credibly mundane fortune teller, and throughout there is a nice balance of the chillingly supernatural with a sharply observed contemporary England peopled by vividly painted characters...some lovely idiosyncratic touches and descriptions." *Shena Mackay*

"Subtly written but still a page-turner, it is a spine-chillingly enjoyable read." *The Lady*

"…strange but appealing…" *Herald Scotland*

"…an interesting and unusual story. I enjoyed the blend of mystery and supernatural. It's quite the page-turner but it doesn't neglect character and detail. Absorbing and evocative, *The Green Door* is a truly enjoyable read." *The Bookbag*

The Purple Shadow

In the years before the war, Sylvie Charlot was a leading light in Paris fashion with many friends among musicians, artists and writers. Now she is largely forgotten. Spending time in Paris during a break in his acting career, Colin Mallory sees a striking portrait of Sylvie. Some think it is a late work by Édouard Vuillard but there is no signature or documentary evidence to support this view.

The picture has some unusual qualities, not least the presence of a shadow of something that cannot be seen. Perhaps the picture was once larger. Colin feels an odd sense of connection with Sylvie, who seems to be looking at him, appealing to him, wanting to tell him something. Despite a warning not to pursue his interest in her portrait, he is determined to find out more about the painting, who painted it, and why it was hidden for many years.

Colin's search takes him back to the film and theatre worlds of Paris and London in the 1930s – and to a house in present-day Sussex. As he uncovers the secrets of Sylvie's past, her portrait seems to take on a life of its own.

"A compelling read. You're drawn into the narrative immediately by the vivid description of a startlingly captivating painting and, as a reader, you're as invested in getting to the bottom of the mystery as the main character is. Bowden is a sharp observer and I loved his descriptions of Paris and London and Sussex and the people who live in both city and country. The novel also spends time describing the lives of jobbing actors and the British film industry in the 1930s. This may be fiction but you feel, as you read, that it comes from a place of knowledge." *The Bookbag*

"Full of idiosyncratic touches and descriptions, this is a story that will keep you guessing." *France magazine*

"Christopher Bowden has again created an intriguing, literary tale with a well-drawn cast of characters. Actor Colin Mallory from *The Red House* can't help but investigate a mysterious painting. The descriptive quality of the writing takes you to the back streets of Paris, and lets you really feel you are solving the mystery hand in hand with Colin." *Lovereading*

The Amber Maze

While staying in a Dorset cottage, Hugh Mullion finds a mysterious key down the side of an antique chair. No one can say how long the key has been there or what it opens.

Hugh's search for answers will unlock the secrets of the troubled life of a talented artist, destined to be hailed a neglected genius fifty years too late. And no secret is darker than that of *The Amber Maze,* from whose malign influence he never escaped.

The trail takes Hugh from Edwardian Oxfordshire to 1960s Camden Town, where the ghosts of the past are finally laid to rest.

"A superbly written mystery that will keep the reader guessing. A finalist and highly recommended." *The Wishing Shelf Book Awards 2019*

"Cleverly plotted and paced. It's a mystery that unlocks the secrets of the past by illuminating and revealing real people with real trials and tribulations. A gentle and elegant dissection, delicately done.
 "A nicely drawn and engaging noirish novel. I thoroughly enjoyed it." *The Bookbag*

"A quietly compelling read which is as much about the journey of discovery as the actual mystery contained within. Following on ten years after *The Blue Book* Hugh Mullion discovers a key down the side of a chair cushion and begins to search for answers. A maze sits centre stage, oppressive, dominating, yet reflected beautifully in the art surrounding it.

"*The Amber Maze* sits as a standalone short novel and you certainly don't have to have read Hugh's previous adventure to start here. Christopher Bowden encourages a simple, almost diary like feel to bring to life the past, as Hugh unravels the mystery in the present. *The Amber Maze* is a considered, intriguing mystery which unfolds at a gentle pace." *Lovereading*

Mr Magenta

Stephen Marling thought he knew his aunt Flora. But when he inherits her house in a quiet south London square a series of discoveries among her papers brings to light another person entirely. Who, for example, is 'Mr Magenta' and what part did he play in her life?

In the process of uncovering the secrets of one life, Stephen is forced to re-evaluate his own and decide what he really wants. Was he right to turn his back on Nancy Steiner, the young actress he met in New York, when he came home to take up his inheritance?

Interweaving past and present, the story takes him from a Brooklyn bookshop to a theatre in Marseille to a cottage on the east coast of England where the truth about Mr Magenta is finally revealed.

"A very original writer."
Charles Harris, best-selling author of Room 15

"As ever, Bowden has written a thoughtful and introspective novel, with a real writer's awareness for the intimate details in people's lives – the ones that feel ordinary and everyday but are often deeply meaningful and pivotal to paths taken and not taken. The narrative runs through the present in London, the recent past in New York, and the further back in Marseille. A love of books and acting and performance permeates every page, which is deeply appealing to a book lover like me.

"There is a good cast of well-rounded characters and Stephen is a patient and reflective investigator so we have plenty of time to savour the noirish aspects of the mystery of Mr Magenta and why he was such a significant character in Flora's life and both the joys and sadnesses that filled it. Suffice it to say that the direction of travel is very often the one you least expect.

"Absorbing, interesting, and with plenty of twists and turns to keep interest levels up, *Mr Magenta* is a fine read, up to the standards we have come to expect from Christopher Bowden." *The Bookbag*